Out of Sight

Robert Rayner

James Lorimer & Company Ltd., Publishers
Toronto

James Lorimer & Company Ltd. acknowledges the support of the Ontario Arts Council. We acknowledge the support of the Government of Canada through the Book Publishing Industry Development Program (BPIDP) for our publishing activities. We acknowledge the support of the Canada Council for the Arts for our publishing program. We acknowledge the support of the Government of Ontario through the Ontario Media Development Corporation's Ontario Book Initiative.

Cover illustration: Greg Ruhl

Library and Archives Canada Cataloguing in Publication

Rayner, Robert, 1946-
    Out of sight / Robert Rayner.

ISBN-10: 1-55028-919-5 (bound);
ISBN-13: 978-1-55028-919-0 (bound)
ISBN-10: 1-55028-918-7 (pbk.); ISBN-13: 978-1-55028-918-3 (pbk.)

    I. Title.
PS8585.A974O98 2006   jC813'.6   C2006-902189-9

James Lorimer & Company Ltd.,
Publishers
317 Adelaide Street West
Suite 1002
Toronto, ON M5V 1P9
www.lorimer.ca

Distributed in the United States by:
Orca Book Publishers
P.O. Box 468
Custer, WA USA
98240-0468

Printed and bound in Canada.

Contents

Acknowledgements

Thanks to Dr. Arnold Brown for his advice on eye diseases; Jennifer Keith of Soccer New Brunswick for her technical advice; and Caira Clark, Edie Brewer, and Nancy Rayner for reading and responding to an early draft of this book.

For Claire

1

Blurry

The soccer ball was a spiralling confusion of black and white. Linh-Mai squinted as the blurry shape fizzed across the wet grass toward her. She had to intercept, because it was her job as fullback to protect the goal.

She swung her foot with the ball, skilfully softening the impact, stopping it against her boot. Now its black-and-white panels were sharp against the vivid green of the soccer field. She could even read what was written on it: *First Division Premium Match Ball. Size 5. FIFA Approved.* But when she looked toward the halfway line, everything blurred again, like an out-of-focus photograph, and she could tell her teammates from the opposition only by their blue Brunswick Valley School uniforms. Someone was calling for the ball, but in the gloomy light of the late fall afternoon she couldn't tell who it was.

Toby, who played fullback with her, said quietly, "It's Steve — on the right wing."

Linh-Mai shouted, "Steve!" and kicked the ball out.

Brian called, "Linh-Mai, you move up. Toby, stay back."

They obeyed. They always did what their goalkeeper said, because he was Flyin' Brian, the best goalie in the Fundy Schools League, who'd earned his nickname by the way he threw himself around the goal making spectacular saves. As Linh-Mai headed upfield, she sneaked a glance back at him. Although the play was now at the other end of the pitch, he was poised on his goal line, ready for action. Mr. Cunningham, their math teacher, said if Brian concentrated on his work as well as he concentrated on the soccer field, he'd be a straight-A student, but in class his attention always seemed to be on everything except what was being taught. Lately Linh-Mai wondered whether his wayward attention was spreading to the soccer field, because he'd made some uncharacteristic mistakes in goal.

She stopped near the halfway line, watching as someone on her team got the ball. She thought it was Steve, the centre forward, or perhaps Shay, the captain. Now her best friend, Julie — she knew it was Julie because she could make out her long, blonde hair flying behind her — was running for a pass, and had slipped the ball to one of the twins, Jillian or Jessica. It was no good trying to decide which one. It was hard to tell them apart even close up.

Jillian — or Jessica — tried a shot, which the Westfield goalkeeper caught easily. He took a few quick steps and kicked the ball out to the wing. The home centre forward burst through a melee of players and chased after it.

Linh-Mai looked behind her. Toby was already moving out to cover the centre forward's approach to goal. Linh-Mai retreated and stationed herself behind him in order to form a second line of defence. Brunswick Valley had been leading Westfield Ridge Middle School by a single goal since early in the first half and she didn't want anyone to get through the defence now, with only ten minutes left in the game. As Toby prepared to tackle, the Westfield centre chipped the ball over him and toward the goal. Linh-Mai narrowed her eyes, trying to get it in focus. From the corner of her eye, she saw Brian on his goal line. He always told his defenders to leave high, easy shots like that for him unless they were sure they could intercept cleanly and keep possession. Although he didn't shout his usual command — "Keeper's!" — she let the ball pass her. It would be an easy save for a goalkeeper as good as Brian. She turned confidently to watch him catch the ball.

But he was weaving his head from side to side, squinting as if the sun was shining in his face. At the last moment, she saw his eyes fix on the ball, but by then it was too late. It slipped through his grasping hands, grazed his shoulder, and bounced into the net.

A few minutes later, with the score still even, the referee whistled for the end of the game.

2

Glasses

The only thing that worried Linh-Mai about having to wear glasses was that she was afraid she might not be allowed to play soccer in them.

That and looking like a dork.

She glanced through the optometrist's big display window, wishing the blind was closed so the people passing on Brunswick Street couldn't see in. Trying on glasses at Dr. Brown's office on a Saturday morning was like getting dressed in public.

She turned from the mirror, deciding she didn't like the frames she had on any more than the seven pairs she'd already tried, and saw Jenna outside — Jenna, who was in her grade seven class at Brunswick Valley School and who always looked as if she'd just stepped out of the "What's Hot" pages of *Teen Flair* magazine, with her long, chestnut hair intricately braided, and her boot-cut jeans, and her cropped tops, and her belly ring. Linh-Mai guessed Jenna's usual entourage wouldn't be far away — and there they were, a group of boys and girls, also from grade seven, scuffling and giggling close behind. Cory and Kyle, who practically panted over Jenna, were among them, of course.

Linh-Mai took the glasses off quickly, but not quickly enough. Kyle, seeing her, said something to Cory, and together they peered in the window, their hands cupped against the glass. Kyle pointed at Linh-Mai, grinning. He made circles with his thumbs and forefingers and placed them around his eyes. Cory did the same.

Dr. Brown gestured angrily at them and closed the blind, but not before Linh-Mai saw the boys call to Jenna and point in the window, laughing.

"Put them on again," Dr. Brown urged. He folded his arms, considering, and said, "They look very nice."

"You look sweet in them," Linh-Mai's mother added. "They suit you."

Linh-Mai didn't say anything. She looked at herself in the mirror and thought — I look like a freak. The frames were black and square. "Do you have anything … colourful?" she asked Dr. Brown.

"Colourful?" he said doubtfully.

Linh-Mai nodded. She thought of Miss Little, her soccer coach, who wore big, round glasses with red frames, and said, "Like … red, perhaps?"

Dr. Brown was burly and bald, except for his bushy side-burns, and he raised his eyebrows behind his thin, gold spectacles and looked at Linh-Mai's mother, who said, "Are you sure, dear?"

Linh-Mai nodded again.

"Well, there's the Uptown Gal collection," said Dr. Brown uncertainly. "We don't sell many of them. The styles are a little — er — flashy, and they seem to be popular only with young women who are … well, flamboyant."

Mrs. Nguyen — a stockier, taller version of her daughter — told Linh-Mai firmly, "You're not the flamboyant type, dear."

She removed her chunky, brown glasses and polished them as she spoke.

Linh-Mai didn't have to be told that. She was probably the least flamboyant person she knew. She thought her best friend, Julie, was sort of flamboyant, in a nice way, and although she didn't wear glasses, Linh-Mai suspected that if Julie did, she'd choose something from the Uptown Gal collection. And Miss Little was definitely flamboyant, with her long, brightly coloured dresses, and her long, blonde hair, and her blue eyes — behind the big, red, round glasses.

Dr. Brown hesitated, glancing at Mrs. Nguyen, who shrugged. He swung open another display panel, revealing a sign that announced in flowery script, *Glasses for the Uptown Gal*. Beneath the sign were rows of spectacles, some with big, square frames, some delicate and narrow, some shaped like cats' eyes, some long and elliptical. Their colours ranged from bright and garish to delicate pastel. Linh-Mai's pointing finger travelled along the rows, lingering at a round, red pair, like Miss Little's, before moving on, pausing, moving on again, returning — and stopping.

"Them," she said. "May I try them, please?"

The glasses were rimless and tinted a dusky red, supported by delicate arms of dull gold.

Dr. Brown glanced at Mrs. Nguyen again.

She frowned. "Do you think they suit you, dear?"

"Don't know."

Dr. Brown slotted the spectacles carefully behind Linh-Mai's ears and settled them on her nose. He stepped back, appraising, leaned forward and adjusted them, leaned back again, head on one side. He smiled. "Well now!"

Mrs. Nguyen, looking at Linh-Mai, smiled, too. "They look great. Your dad will love them."

Mr. Nguyen was an information technology consultant and was away for three months working for a company in Toronto. He wore glasses, too — square, rimless ones that Linh-Mai thought made him look smart and efficient.

Linh-Mai turned to the mirror. Her black eyes looked mysterious behind the tinted lenses, and the dull gold arms glittered against her black, shoulder-length hair.

"You're not wearing them for soccer, young lady," Mrs. Nguyen warned.

"I may not even be allowed to play soccer if I'm wearing glasses," Linh-Mai grumbled.

"They're shatterproof," Dr. Brown said quickly. "They'd be fine for sports. Of course you'd need to secure them." He pulled open a little drawer under the display rack and produced a wide, vivid red, elastic strap. He took the glasses from Linh-Mai, attached the strap, and replaced them, adjusting the elastic around her head.

She looked in the mirror again. Her hair was pinned tightly above the strap, but bunched outward beneath it. She thought she looked like a comic book hero, or some kind of warrior.

"Please, Mom?" she said.

"They look expensive," Mrs. Nguyen said cautiously.

Dr. Brown shook his head emphatically. "No more than the others."

Linh-Mai tried again. "*Please*, Mom?"

"I guess they'll be all right," said Mrs. Nguyen.

Linh-Mai hugged her.

"What do you call this style?" Mrs. Nguyen asked Dr. Brown.

He cleared his throat and murmured, "Mystical Allure."

Mrs. Nguyen raised her eyebrows.

Linh-Mai grinned.

3

Brian

On Monday morning Linh-Mai dressed for school in her usual grey jeans and black sweater.

She sat for a moment, as she did every morning, to study the photo on her bedside table. It showed her parents; her father slim and neat in his business suit, her mother, the same height as her husband but a little broader, wearing a loose, shiny, flowery dress. She wished her father didn't have to go away as often as he did, although when he returned he always brought her something, a book about soccer, a signed team photo if he'd been in one of the cities that hosted a Canadian Soccer League team, even a soccer shirt in the colours of those teams. She already had four, which she wore in turn on the weekends.

She made a final check of her homework and glanced through her social studies notes in preparation for the test she'd have to write in period two. She packed her books into her backpack, texts at the front, scribblers behind.

With everything ready, she opened the red case containing her new glasses. Facing away from her mirror, she took them out and placed the arms carefully behind her ears. She moved the spectacles backwards and forwards on her nose until they were comfortable. She straightened her arms by her sides and clenched her fists.

She turned to the mirror.

They looked all right, she told herself firmly, and it didn't matter what anyone — anyone like Cory and Kyle — said about them. Besides, she was used to being teased at school, about her good marks, about always having her work done, about being younger and smaller than the rest of the class. The glasses would be just one more thing to taunt her with.

But still, she couldn't help worrying as she left for school. She walked with her mother through the subdivision where they lived — a network of white, boxy houses and trimmed lawns — and swung on to wide Riverside Drive, which had big, old houses set back from the road on one side, and on the other the river that wound through the little town of Brunswick Valley.

They stopped at the end of the street, at Brian's house, and Mrs. Nguyen asked, "Are you coming in?"

Mrs. Nguyen worked for Brian's father, who had a construction company. Her office was in Mr. Price's house, and Linh-Mai often stopped there on her way to school. Brian was in Linh-Mai's grade seven class and she always hoped he might walk the rest of the way to school with her.

Mr. Price was sitting at the kitchen table, with papers strewn around the remains of his breakfast. He was singing to himself as he pored over them: "Don't expect a time of ease, 'cause life's a mean and fickle tease. It promises, then takes away. That's why I sit and cry today."

He stopped singing and mumbled, "Morning, ladies. Help me sort out these invoices, please, Mrs. N."

Mrs. Nguyen said, "I'll get the files," and went into her office, a tiny room off the kitchen.

Shuffling papers, Mr. Price said to Linh-Mai, "How's my favourite daughter — the one I never had?" He looked up. "Hey — I like the glasses. *Très élégant*."

His hair was curly and unkempt, the colour of fresh cedar shingles, and his eyes sparkled in his round, friendly face. His baggy sweater, to which a few wood chips always clung, made his shoulders seem even broader than they already were. He reminded Linh-Mai of a big, friendly dog. Once she'd asked Brian where Mrs. Price was, and he'd shrugged and said, "She went somewhere when I was little. I don't remember her."

Linh-Mai asked, "Is Brian ready?"

"Are you kidding?" said Mr. Price. "I've called him three times since I woke him up and I still haven't laid eyes on him." He shouted, "Brian!"

From somewhere upstairs Brian answered, "What?"

"Are you ready?"

"Ready for what?"

"For school, of course. What do you think?"

"Why?"

"Because it's time to go and Linh-Mai's here asking if you're ready so the two of you can walk down to school together." He looked at Linh-Mai. "Right, dear?"

Linh-Mai nodded.

"I can't find my math book," Brian shouted.

Linh-Mai couldn't help smiling, even though she knew Brian's state of constant disorganization, and his short attention span, drove his father, as well as his teachers, crazy. She pointed to the counter beside the sink, where the math book lay among dirty dishes, a crumpled newspaper, two cartons of milk, and more invoices.

Mr. Price rolled his eyes. "It's here — where you threw it when you came home on Friday."

A thunder of feet sounded on the stairs and Brian burst through the door. He slid across the kitchen on his knees, with his arms out, as if he'd just scored a goal in the World Cup. His grey eyes sparkled like his father's, and his thick hair, the same cedar colour as Mr. Price's, was a tousled mess. He was wearing jeans and a pajama top.

"Your book's here," Mr. Price repeated.

"What book?" said Brian. He rose from the floor in a smooth, easy motion, took a piece of toast from the table and poured a glass of orange juice. He was nearly as tall as his father.

Mr. Price muttered, "Give me strength."

"Why?" said Brian.

"I said your math book — the one you were looking for — is here."

He pointed. Brian peered uncertainly at the counter, squinting. Linh-Mai passed him the book. She looked directly at him, waiting for him to comment on her glasses. She had planned to tell him about them, but something had stopped her. She wanted him to notice her, but not just because she was wearing new glasses. She wanted him to notice her as a person.

"Oh!" said Brian, "thanks," and he tucked the book under his arm.

Mr. Price asked, "Did you do your math homework?"

"What math homework?" said Brian.

"The math homework you were complaining about on Friday when you threw your math book on the counter."

Brian reflected. "I don't know."

Mr. Price sighed. "You better hurry and get yourself ready for school."

"I'm ready," said Brian.

"You're wearing your pajamas," said Mr. Price.

Linh-Mai giggled.

"I'm not," said Brian. He looked down. "Okay, just the top." He finished his toast and juice, lobbed the math book in the air in front of him, and jumped to catch it. He put the book on his head and balanced it there, holding his arms out. Looking through the window, he said, "There are two goldfinches at the feeder, but I don't think there's much seed in it."

Mr. Price started, "Brian …"

"Shall I fill it before I go?"

"Brian!"

"What?"

"Get ready for school."

"I am ready."

Mr. Price pointed at Brian's pajama top.

Brian looked at it as if he'd never seen it before. "I'll put my shirt on."

"Good idea," said Mr. Price, as Brian barged from the room.

Mrs. Nguyen emerged from her office with a pile of files. She looked at Linh-Mai, "If you want to get to school on time, you'd better hurry."

With a glance up the stairs where Brian had bounded, Linh-Mai reluctantly said, "See you later."

"Suppose you could help him out a bit in math class?" said Mr. Price.

Linh-Mai nodded. "I'll try."

"You're a sweetheart," said Mr. Price.

As she left the house, the sound of bird song caught Linh-Mai's attention. She looked at the feeder, smiling as she remembered when Brian had wanted to feed the goldfinches instead of getting ready for school. She looked more carefully. The birds at the feeder were chickadees, and there was no sign of goldfinches. She wondered briefly how Brian could confuse two such different birds.

4

School

At school she walked across the crowded playground with her head down, and no one seemed to notice her, or her new glasses. Linh-Mai often felt invisible, and she was grateful for that today.

Jenna was in the middle of a group of students lounging on the steps in front of the door. Kyle and Cory stood beside her.

Kyle called loudly in a singsong voice, "Linh-Mai's got new glasses," and Cory commented, "She looks dorkier than ever."

As Linh-Mai walked through the group, ignoring the taunts, she caught Jenna's eye.

Jenna smiled and said, "My aunt has glasses like that."

Linh-Mai hesitated. "Really?"

Jenna nodded. "She got them at the dollar store."

Linh-Mai pushed through the door as the group around Jenna laughed. Kyle and Cory followed her inside, fingers around their eyes, pretending to peer around through thick glasses.

Toby was in the hallway, reading a notice on the soccer bulletin board. He looked around and said, "Quit it, you guys."

"Who says?" Kyle challenged.

Shay stepped from behind Toby's bulky frame and added quietly, "Toby and me that's who says. So butt out."

Linh-Mai looked gratefully at her friends Shay, compact and sturdy, and Toby, big, loose and flabby. She was still shy of them, despite knowing them from soccer, because she was a newcomer to the class, and was younger than them. She'd been unexpectedly promoted to grade seven only a few weeks ago, in the middle of September, skipping a grade because her marks were so high. The principal had told her parents she was gifted, but Linh-Mai had begged them not to tell anyone. She was comfortable with the work in her new grade, but felt like a social misfit. The girls, like Jenna, seemed so sophisticated and experienced, with their stylish clothes and their endless talk about boys and boyfriends. And the boys seemed so loud and boisterous — except for serious Shay, with his nice, old-fashioned gallantry, and wisecracking, good-natured, teaseable Toby. She wasn't sure where Brian fit in. Although he was often louder and more boisterous than the other boys, still, something set him apart from them. His antics seemed part of him, somehow innocent, and not put on to impress or intimidate.

Kyle and Cory scuttled back to Jenna.

"Jerks," said Toby dismissively.

Shay and Toby looked at Linh-Mai. She looked down.

After a few seconds of silence, Shay said awkwardly, "You've got them."

She'd told Shay she was getting glasses because he was captain of the soccer team and she was afraid she wouldn't be allowed to play in them. And she'd told Toby because he played fullback with her. The only other people who knew were Julie, because she was Linh-Mai's best friend, and Miss Little, because she was coach.

Linh-Mai kept her head down.

"They're cool," Shay added quickly.

"Yeah, right," muttered Linh-Mai.

"They are — really," said Toby.

Linh-Mai raised her head and whispered, "Really?"

"They make you look … smart," said Toby.

Linh-Mai smiled and murmured, "Thanks." Then she caught herself and looked up at Toby's grinning face. "So how did I look before?"

He chuckled, then pirouetted clumsily in the hallway, demanding, "*Now* do you see?"

"See what?" said Linh-Mai.

"How good-looking I am," said Toby.

Linh-Mai giggled. "Idiot."

Then she heard running footsteps. Julie flew down the hallway, skidded to a halt, and demanded, "Let's see them." She put her hands on Linh-Mai's shoulders, gazing at the new glasses. Like Shay and Toby, she was a head taller than Linh-Mai. They often joked that Linh-Mai was the baby on the soccer team because she was the smallest as well as the youngest. Her friends were thirteen, but Linh-Mai was still only twelve.

"They're *brilliant*," Julie breathed. "They're shatterproof — right? So they'll be okay for soccer?"

Linh-Mai said, "I hope so. Miss Little's checking the league rules."

Shay pointed to the notice on the bulletin board. "There's a practice at noon, to get ready for the game with St. Croix after school."

Toby said, "I love the playoffs."

"Me too," said Linh-Mai.

She liked the excitement of the fiercely contested games, which came at the end of the regular Fundy Schools League season and determined which teams would represent the province in the Maritime Schools Summer Games the following year. Brunswick Valley had been drawn in a group with St. Croix Middle School and Westfield Ridge Middle School, and they had to play one another at home and away. Only one team from each group would go to the Summer Games. The tie with Westfield Ridge had been Brunswick Valley's first game of the playoffs.

Shay said wistfully, "I'd like them more if we'd made a better start. We should have beaten Westfield Ridge."

"We'll win the playoffs," Toby announced confidently. They all looked at him, and he pointed to a banner hanging further down the hallway. "All we have to do is dream it."

Everyone groaned.

The banner promised, *If you can dream it — then you can do it!* There were posters and banners like it all over the school, left behind by an inspirational speaker who had visited their classroom the previous week. Before the visit a glossy poster had promised: *Myrna Spigot — Olympic swimmer at the age of only seventeen!* However, when questioned, Myrna Spigot had revealed that she had swum only in practice sessions at the Olympics, as a reserve for the synchronized swimming team. No one had taken the inspirational speaker, or her message, very seriously.

Shay said, "It'll take more than dreaming for us to beat St. Croix."

"It'd help if Brian got his act together,' said Julie. "I don't know what's wrong with him."

Linh-Mai glanced back and saw Brian on the steps outside. He was talking to Jenna. Linh-Mai adjusted her glasses and raised her hand in a little wave. Brian seemed to look right at her, before turning his attention back to Jenna. Linh-Mai felt a stab of hurt, or jealousy, or anger; she wasn't sure which. As they all headed off to class, Linh-Mai remembered Brian's strange mistake in goal, and how he couldn't see where his math book was until she had passed it to him, and his confusion over the goldfinches and the chickadees. She thought: Perhaps he really didn't see me. Does he need glasses, too?

5

Practice

When Linh-Mai arrived for soccer practice on the back field, Miss Little greeted her with, "I *love* your glasses, and the strap is *gorgeous*."

Linh-Mai ducked her head, flushing with pleasure at Miss Little's compliment. She mumbled, "Have you … did you …"

"I couldn't find anything in the league rules about wearing glasses for soccer," said Miss Little. "But I called the league president, and she says the latest bulletin from the Canadian Soccer Association leaves it to the match officials to give players permission to wear glasses — if they think they're safe. So I'm sure it will be okay."

She blew her whistle and the team gathered around her — all except Brian, who was swinging from the crossbar of the goal.

She called, "Brian."

He kept swinging.

Linh-Mai thought how strange it was that most times, Brian's attention flitted from one thing to another, never settling anywhere for more than a few seconds, while at other times it was so focused it shut out everything else. Like when he was in goal, when nothing seemed to exist for him except the ball and the way everyone on the field moved in relation to it. Right now she could tell he was focused so completely on swinging from the crossbar that he couldn't even hear Miss Little, who called again, "Brian!"

Brian swung on intently.

Miss Little shouted again and blew a piercing whistle blast.

Brian released the crossbar and dropped to the ground. "What?"

"We're waiting for you."

"Sorry, Miss Little." He jogged across to join the group.

Miss Little shook her head and continued, "Last night St. Croix Middle School tied with Westfield Ridge for the second time. So, with a point for each tied game, and four goals, they're above us, because we have only one point and one goal from our tie with Westfield Ridge. But if we can beat St. Croix this afternoon and earn three points, we'll move above them in the round robin table."

"We would have beaten Westfield if Brian hadn't let that goal in," grumbled Steve, Brunswick Valley's stocky centre forward. He had a mat of coarse, sandy hair that hung to his shoulders and fell in a fringe to his eyebrows.

"I misjudged the flight of the ball," said Brian. He scuffed the ground with his soccer cleats.

"Of course you misjudged the flight of the ball," Steve retorted. "You weren't even looking at it until it nearly knocked you over."

"That's enough," said Miss Little.

"I was … it was … the sun was in my eyes," said Brian.

"It was cloudy," Steve muttered.

"The goal was no one's fault," said Miss Little, looking hard at Steve. "Let's forget about it and concentrate on today's game."

"Hear that, Brian?" said Steve. "Concentrate. That means

watching the ball."

Miss Little snapped, "Steve!"

Brian mumbled, "Wasn't my fault."

Miss Little went on, "Now Shay has something to tell you that will help if you have to tackle one of the St. Croix forwards."

Shay started, "You remember their two strikers, Casey Dougan and John Hawler …"

"Hawler the Mauler," Julie put in.

Linh-Mai remembered John Hawler, St. Croix's big, rough centre forward. He was known as the Mauler because he used his elbows to push defenders out of his way, and his feet to kick them as much as the ball. Linh-Mai thought he fouled a lot, but he seemed to get away with it most of the time.

Shay continued, "Hawler always shoots with his right foot and sends the ball left, and Dougan always shoots with his left foot, and sends the ball right." He turned to Brian. "They do that if it's a penalty kick, too — and if St. Croix gets a penalty kick, you can be sure one of them will take it."

Brian nodded. "It'd probably be Hawler. He's the best."

Linh-Mai repeated to herself, as if learning something for a test: Hawler — right foot, shoots left; Dougan — left foot, shoots right.

Miss Little said, "Our best chance of a goal against St. Croix will be on the breakaway, so we'll practise turning defence into attack. Brian will start the move with a long kick upfield to Steve and the twins."

Jillian and Jessica, who played on the wings, nodded, their ponytails swinging in unison.

Miss Little went on, "Then one of the forwards will gather the ball and pass it straight on for another to shoot."

She handed the ball to Brian. "I'll go in the other goal so I can send the ball back for you to start the move again."

Miss Little jogged to the other end of the pitch. Linh-Mai took up a position a short way upfield, with Toby beside her. The forwards and midfielders spread out near Miss Little's goal.

"Ready, Brian?" Miss Little called. "First, kick the ball out to Jessica."

Brian trotted to the edge of the penalty area, dropped the ball to his feet, and in a smooth motion kicked it on the half volley. Linh-Mai watched it soar to the other end of the field and land at Jillian's feet. Surprised, Jillian scrambled to trap it.

Miss Little laughed. "Wrong twin, Brian."

"I thought you could tell them apart," Toby commented.

"I can," Brian mumbled. "I just didn't look properly."

"Try again," said Miss Little.

Brian kicked the ball out and it landed at Jessica's feet. She passed quickly to Steve, who shot past Miss Little into the net.

Miss Little said, "This time we'll have Steve and Shay on the wings and the twins in the middle." Shay and Steve jogged to the wings and the twins moved inside as Miss Little kicked the ball to Brian and called, "Try a pass to Shay." A few moments later, she prompted, "We're ready, Brian."

Linh-Mai looked behind her. Brian was bouncing the ball while he looked upfield. His eyes were roving between Shay and Steve. Following his gaze, Linh-Mai realized the boys were the same height and had the same compact, sturdy build, and similarly coloured hair. The only differences — she could make them out only because she was wearing her new glasses — were that Steve had a pouty mouth and widely spaced eyes, while Shay had even features, and his hair was shorter.

Brian was still bouncing the ball.

Linh-Mai said quietly, "Shay's on the left wing."

Brian looked briefly at her, then kicked the ball effortlessly to the feet of Shay.

6

Class

Linh-Mai looked happily at the fractions Mr. Cunningham was writing on the chalkboard. From her desk near the back of the room she could read them easily. She allowed her eyes to wander upward to the banner strung across the wall at the front of the class: *If you can dream it — then you can do it!* She could read that easily, too. As she copied the fractions neatly and mechanically into her exercise book, she recalled a little guiltily how they'd made fun of their guest speaker and her message. After Myrna Spigot had told the class how she had achieved her dream of taking part in the Olympic Games, she'd asked the students to share their dreams with her. When no one volunteered, she said she'd choose someone. Linh-Mai knew she'd choose Julie. Visitors to the class always did. Linh-Mai thought it was something to do with how she looked like a fairy-tale princess. Gazing at Julie, Myrna Spigot had asked breathlessly, "What do you dream of being?" and Julie had said a wrestler on WWE. Then Myrna Spigot had tried Steve, and he'd said a hit man. She'd turned in desperation to Toby, who was sprawled in his seat, bulky and graceless, and when he said he dreamed of being a ballet dancer, it had taken Mr. Cunningham's intervention to restore order.

Linh-Mai suppressed a smile at the memory, and forced her attention back to her work. It was the first class of the afternoon, and no one seemed to notice her glasses anymore.

Mr. Cunningham was short and thickset, and his bushy black eyebrows met in the middle. Now he turned to the class and announced, "Here are some more fractions to multiply. You can start them now and finish tonight. Then I'll mark these examples with last Friday's homework."

Linh-Mai thought, now Brian has another chance to get his homework done. Perhaps I can help him. She pictured herself beside him at the kitchen table after school, Brian bent over his math book, while she pointed to figures. But she knew he wouldn't sit still long enough for that to happen. The best she could do was let him copy her work.

Across the aisle from her, Brian's desk was bare. He was leaning back, his chair on two legs, his eyes closed, his head bobbing with the rhythm he was drumming with his forefingers on the edge of his desk.

Mr. Cunningham had resumed writing on the chalkboard. Without looking around he paused and said "You are getting these fractions down, aren't you, Brian?"

Brian stopped drumming, opened his eyes, lowered his chair, and said, "Yes, Mr. C."

"Good," said Mr. Cunningham. "So when I look around in a moment I will see your book on your desk and a pencil in your hand, won't I?"

"Right on, Mr. C.," said Brian.

Linh-Mai watched as Brian rummaged briefly in his desk. Before he removed anything from it, his attention shifted to the window, through which a flock of gulls was visible, swooping down to the playground in search of scraps left behind after recess. A few seconds later he turned his attention to a grass stain on the knee of his pants. He picked at it before tilting his chair back again, this time drumming in the air. Linh-Mai allowed herself a moment of exasperation, knowing he'd expect her to help him with anything his antics caused him to miss, but still she couldn't help smiling at him when he caught her eye and grinned as he pushed his chair further back. The legs slipped and he crashed to the ground. Mr. Cunningham spun around.

Brian jumped up. "Sorry, Mr. C. My chair slipped."

Mr. Cunningham said, "Was it the result of your attention slipping, too?"

"Oh no, Mr. C.," said Brian, reaching into his desk for his exercise book and a pencil. "The floor's slippery."

Jenna, sitting at the desk in front of Brian, turned and whispered, "Idiot." She grinned.

Brian winked at her.

Linh-Mai looked away, but a moment later, as the class settled back to work, she couldn't resist watching as Brian took his steel ruler from his desk and inched it toward Jenna's back, where a sliver of skin was showing between her low-rise jeans and her short T-shirt as she leaned forward in her desk. She stirred in her seat and Brian froze. Linh-Mai knew Jenna's clothes came from Les Teens Sensuelles in the mall, because she'd seen the same outfit in the window. Mrs. Nguyen wouldn't allow her even to enter, let alone shop at, Les Teens Sensuelles. She said the clothes they sold there were an invitation to "get up to no good." She never explained what getting up to no good involved, but Linh-Mai could guess. She shook her head and returned to her work. A few seconds later she was mesmerized again as Brian continued sliding his ruler stealthily forward. At the last moment he turned it on its edge and pressed the flat side of the cold steel against Jenna's bare skin.

She shrieked and whirled around. "Cut it out, Brian!"

Mr. Cunningham paused his writing and turned to the class. "What's going on?"

Everyone looked toward the back of the class, where Brian held his arms out, eyes wide with innocence.

"He put his cold fingers down my back," Jenna said.

She looked round at Brian, and she was grinning.

Brian grinned at Jenna. "Didn't."

Jenna turned back toward Mr. Cunningham, her face suddenly expressing hurt and outrage.

"He did."

"Did you, Brian?"

"Did I what?"

Mr. Cunningham sighed. "Did you put your cold fingers down Jenna's back?"

"No."

Jenna exploded. "You *did*, Brian!"

"The truth, please, Brian," Mr. Cunningham insisted.

"I put my *ruler* down her back," Brian explained patiently.

"Would you join me at the front of the room, please?" the teacher said.

"What's up, Mr. C.?" said Brian, leaving his desk.

Mr. Cunningham folded his arms. "What's up, Brian, is that this is a mathematics class, not a drumming class, or a let's-see-how-far-I-can-lean-back-in-my-chair-without-it-falling-over class, or a let's-see-how-much-I-can-annoy-Jenna class."

Brian nodded. "Right, Mr. C. Sorry, Mr. C."

"So I'd like you to apologize to Jenna and the class for the disruption, and then return to your seat and concentrate on your mathematics. Okay?"

"Right, Mr. C."

Brian set off for his desk.

Mr. Cunningham asked mildly, "Brian, what did I just tell you to do?"

"You said to return to my seat and concentrate on my mathematics," Brian said confidently.

"Before that," said Mr. Cunningham.

Brian frowned, biting his lip in concentration.

"Mere seconds — mere *nanoseconds* — before that," Mr. Cunningham prompted.

Brian thought deeply. "Can't remember, Mr. C."

Mr. Cunningham sighed again. He waved Brian away and told the class, "Now that the Brian and Jenna show is finished, can we all please get back to work?"

Jenna turned to Brian as he sat back at his desk. She tossed her head, whispered, "Jerk," and grinned.

Brian grinned back.

Linh-Mai looked away, gritting her teeth, wondering bitterly whether she should call him a jerk, too, just supposing she could summon the nerve, so that he'd grin like that at her. But even as she thought it, she knew she'd never do it, not just because she didn't have the nerve, but also because she knew he wasn't being a jerk when he pulled his classroom stunts. He was just being … Brian. She'd watched him carefully enough to know he simply couldn't control his wandering attention, which seized on whatever attracted it most from one second to the next, whether it was seagulls, or the sound of drums in his head, or Jenna's bare back.

7

Hero and Villain

After school, Linh-Mai hurried to Mr. Price's house, where she changed into her blue Brunswick Valley School soccer uniform in her mother's little office. She'd hoped to walk over with Brian, but as soon as classes ended he fell into conversation with Jenna, so Linh-Mai didn't want to hang around. Mrs. Morton, Toby's mother, was giving them a ride to St. Croix for the game and Linh-Mai worried about keeping her waiting.

Brian rushed through the kitchen at the same time as Mrs. Morton pulled up outside.

Linh-Mai said, "Hi, Bri," looking hopefully at him. He hadn't commented on her glasses all day. She thought something teasing, or even some kind of put-down, would be better than nothing.

He said, "Is Dad here?"

Mrs. Nguyen said, "He can't get away from the site. He says to play your best and enjoy the game — both of you — and he'll see you when you get back."

Brian raced upstairs while Linh-Mai went out to the van.

Toby's mother said, "I suppose Brian's not ready."

"He just got home," said Linh-Mai. "He'll be ready soon."

She climbed into the back seat, behind Shay and Julie. Toby was sitting in the front.

Mrs. Morton, who was fair-haired and chubby, like Toby, marched to the back door of the house and shouted, "Brian, get your rear end down here fast!"

He appeared a few minutes later and said, "Are you guys ready?"

"We were about to leave you behind," Mrs. Morton grumbled.

Brian, climbing in and sitting beside Linh-Mai, said, "The team couldn't do without me."

Mrs. Morton shook her head, muttering, "Listen to him."

Linh-Mai thought, but it's true. We couldn't do without him. His goalkeeping has helped us win more times than I can remember.

Mrs. Morton started the van.

Mrs. Nguyen ran from the house and told Brian, "You might find these useful." She handed him his soccer boots.

As they drove into St. Croix, Brian fidgeted in his seat and talked, his words tumbling out. "We're going to win, folks. That Hawler won't get one past me. He didn't score past me last year and he hasn't this year and he won't today. But it's going to be close. They're a good team. I'm going to need Toby and you," he nudged Linh-Mai in the ribs, "on your toes in defence." He held his hands up as if to catch a ball and weaved from side to side, his shoulder brushing against Linh-Mai's, while his feet pattered on the floor of the van. "So get yourselves wound up for a tough game, folks."

"What about you, Brian?" said Mrs. Morton. "Are you wound up?"

"Cool as a cucumber," said Brian.

As soon as Mrs. Morton stopped the van in front of St. Croix Middle School, he wrenched the door open and leaped out, calling, "Let's *go*, folks!"

Mrs. Morton muttered, "Like he was shot from a cannon …"

Linh-Mai put on her cleats in the girls' changing room and stuffed her shin pads into her socks. She settled the strap of her glasses firmly around her head and jogged out through the big doors at the rear of the school. The stone steps led down to the soccer field, which was laid out like a huge lawn behind the two-storey brick building. She paused, looking down at the field. At one end, Steve and the twins were firing shots at goal, while Julie and Shay did stretching exercises behind it, and Toby sprawled on the ground. At the other end the St. Croix players were warming up, among them the intimidating figure of John Hawler. He was taller than anyone on either team, and was rivalled in height only by Casey Dougan and in bulk only by Toby.

Cleats clattered behind her. Brian ran past and started to descend the steps. He stopped, looking uncertainly from one end of the pitch to the other. A cold wind was sweeping across the field and the players were wearing track suit tops or sweaters over their soccer shirts, hiding their team colours, the blue of Brunswick Valley and the purple of St. Croix. Looking too, Linh-Mai realized that unless you recognized individual players, it was impossible to tell one side from the other.

She joined Brian, said, "This way," and set off toward their teammates.

Brian careened past her, saying "I was just seeing what shape the pitch was in."

Linh-Mai muttered, "Right — like you can see anything at all that far away." She really liked Brian, but that was almost eclipsed momentarily by a growing exasperation. Why didn't he simply admit he couldn't see, and do something about it? He could get glasses, like she'd done.

Miss Little and the referee were at the corner of the field, their backs to Linh-Mai. In his uniform of black shirt and shorts, the referee was working at something he held in front of him.

She approached and said quietly, "Excuse me."

The referee turned. He was bowlegged and portly and had white, wispy hair that blew around in fine strands. Leaning toward her, his hands behind his back, he said, "This must be the young lady who's worried about not being allowed to play in her new glasses."

Linh-Mai nodded.

Miss Little said, "This is Referee Cline."

He peered at Linh-Mai's glasses. "Are they shatterproof?"

She nodded again. "Dr. Brown said they'd be all right for soccer."

Referee Cline smiled. "If Dr. Brown said they'd be all right, that's good enough for me." Bringing his hands from behind him, he revealed a pair of glasses with thick lenses, which he'd been polishing with a little cloth. He put them on and said, "I guess Miss Little and you and I have the same problem. We just can't get along without our spectacles."

Linh-Mai said, "So it's all right — I can play in them?"

"Of course you can. And I'll be reffing all your playoff games so you don't have to ask again."

Linh-Mai drew a deep breath of relief, fought down the nerves that always came to her at the start of every game, and joined her teammates on the field.

***

They hardly spoke as Mrs. Morton drove them home.

The only thing Brian said was, "Now St. Croix has five points and we've still only got one. And it's all because of me."

Shay said wearily, "It wasn't your fault, Bri."

Linh-Mai looked at Brian from the corner of her eye. He was unusually still beside her — more still than she'd ever seen him — and his head was hanging down. She wanted to put her hand on his arm and say, "You were brilliant in goal. You saved us — time after time. It's like Miss Little said after the game: We didn't lose 1-0 because of you. We lost by *only* one because of you. You're the hero of the game — although you think you're the villain of it. And it's not your fault we lost. It's mine."

As they sat in silence, she let her mind drift back over the game.

Brian's first big save was in the first minute, when he dived at Hawler's feet and smothered the ball after the St. Croix striker had passed Toby easily and elbowed Linh-Mai aside as she went to tackle him. Then, halfway through the first half, St. Croix had a corner kick and Brian dived for the ball at the same time Hawler swung his foot at it. Brian caught the ball — and Hawler's boot on the side of his head. Linh-Mai was first to reach him as he lay unmoving on the ground, his eyes closed. She wanted to cradle his head, but Toby, rushing up, warned, "Don't move him." Then Brian opened his eyes, grinned, and leaped up. Miss Little and the referee had wanted him to take a time out, but he'd refused.

Soon after that a shot from Hawler bounced off Toby's outstretched leg, and Brian, having already launched himself in the direction of Hawler's kick, somehow twisted in mid-air and tipped the deflection around the post.

As St. Croix maintained a relentless attack, he saved again and again — until two minutes from the end, when Casey

Dougan blasted a shot at the Brunswick Valley goal. Brian dived and parried but couldn't hold on to the ball, which spun to Hawler. Suddenly, Linh-Mai found herself the only one between the St. Croix striker and the goal.

She was approaching cautiously, trying to force Hawler out toward the wing, when he unleashed a ferocious shot that flew toward her face. She had a fleeting image of shattered glasses and instinctively put her hands up to protect herself. The ball smashed against them and deflected past the goal.

Hawler demanded, "Penalty, ref."

Referee Cline hesitated. The St. Croix spectators took up the cry: "Penalty! Penalty!"

Shay protested, "It was self-defence."

The referee said, "I'm sorry — but it was a clear hand ball, and the shot was headed for goal."

Brian, who was still lying where he'd landed after saving the first shot, argued, "I had it covered!"

The referee pointed to the penalty spot.

As the players took their positions on the edge of the goal area in preparation for the kick, Linh-Mai whispered, "Sorry, Brian."

He grinned. "It wasn't your fault. No sweat, anyway. Hawler won't get one past me."

But when the referee placed the ball on the penalty spot, both Hawler and Dougan came forward. Linh-Mai had removed her glasses to check them over. She saw Brian looking from Hawler to Dougan. Linh-Mai looked at them, too. They were both tall and broad, with long, dark brown hair. Without her glasses, she couldn't tell them apart, and with a surge of panic she suddenly understood why Brian was looking from one to the other.

Referee Cline said, "Who's taking the kick?"

The St. Croix forwards conferred.

Linh-Mai recalled: Hawler — right foot shoots left; Dougan — left foot shoots right. But it's no good knowing that if you can't tell who's taking the kick.

She put her glasses on.

Brian was still looking with narrowed eyes from Hawler to Dougan.

Hawler stepped back and Dougan prepared to shoot.

Linh-Mai wondered whether she could call or signal to Brian that it was Casey Dougan, not John Hawler, standing over the ball. She looked to Shay for guidance, but, with Julie and Toby, he was already crouched on the edge of the penalty area, ready to run forward as soon as the kick was taken. She looked back at Brian. Was she the only one who understood his predicament? But even as she wondered, the referee blew his whistle. Dougan trotted forward and fired the ball right.

Brian dived left.

Dougan raised his arms in triumph as the ball hit the back of the net. A few minutes later, with St. Croix still leading 1-0, the referee whistled the end of the game.

As the Brunswick Valley team had left the field, Steve snarled at Brian, "Why d'you dive left when Dougan always shoots right?"

Linh-Mai wanted to answer: Because he couldn't see.

Brian put his head down and muttered, "I wasn't thinking."

Shay, walking beside him, said, "You played a great game, Bri."

Toby walked on his other side, his hand on Brian's shoulder, while Linh-Mai and Julie followed close behind. But not everyone was as supportive.

Jillian said, "You're getting as foolish in goal as you are in class," and Jessica said, "You need to keep your mind on what you're doing."

Steve added bitterly, "Thanks for losing the game for us, Brian."

Linh-Mai wanted to sink into the ground. She knew she'd been the one who'd lost the game because she'd caused the penalty. Brian's only mistake was not admitting he had eye problems.

Miss Little was waiting for them at the side of the field. Her voice was stern, "I don't want to hear any talk about Brian being to blame for the goal. Brian is a hero. I lost count of how many saves he made — and he let in only one goal. If it wasn't for him, we would have lost by ten goals or more." As she spoke, she put her arm round his shoulders, and when the team moved on, she kept it there, detaining him, at the same time as she called, "Linh-Mai, wait, please."

Linh-Mai stayed while the others drifted away.

Miss Little told her firmly, "The goal was not your fault either."

"But I handled the ball."

"You couldn't help that. Now — let me see your glasses. I don't want you going home with them damaged." While she examined them, she said casually to Brian, "Do you suppose wearing glasses would help you in goal?"

Brian looked up quickly. "What do you mean?"

"I mean, would it be a good idea to have your eyes checked to see if you need glasses?"

"Yeah, right. A goalkeeper with glasses. I can just see it."

"They'd be no more of a problem than Linh-Mai wearing them to play."

"Look what happened to her. Anyway, I've never seen a goalkeeper wearing glasses and I'm not going to be the first."

Linh-Mai murmured "It's not so bad, wearing glasses, once you get over wearing them for the first time."

Miss Little suggested gently, "It wouldn't hurt to have your eyes checked."

Brian's voice rose. "There's nothing wrong with my eyes. It's ... it's like the twins said. It's my concentration that's the problem."

He stalked from the field.

Riding home in the van, Linh-Mai brought her mind back to the present, to Brian, sitting beside her in morose silence.

She whispered, "The goal was my fault."

He shook his head.

8

Goalkeepers Don't Wear Glasses

As soon as they stopped at Brian's house, he jumped out without speaking and slammed the van door. Linh-Mai, about to climb out behind him, recoiled. Shay opened the door for her, and Julie said, "He'll get over it." With a murmured "Thank you" to Mrs. Morton, Linh-Mai followed Brian, who had already barged into the house through the back door, slamming that, too.

In the kitchen, he was standing by the door to the stairs, his hands in his pockets, while Mr. Price stood stirring a saucepan on the stove and said, "No, Brian, your supper's ready. You can go up to your room after we've eaten."

Linh-Mai could hear her mother on the telephone in her office.

Brian slumped in a chair at the kitchen table. Linh-Mai leaned against the counter.

Mr. Price said, "So, how did the game go? It was against St. Croix, wasn't it?"

Linh-Mai nodded.

"Was it a good game?"

Linh-Mai shrugged. "Okay."

Mr. Price looked at Brian, still slumped at the table with his head down. Then he looked at Linh-Mai, his eyebrows raised.

Linh-Mai shrugged again.

Mr. Price said, "What about you, Brian?"

Brian mumbled, "What about me?"

"Did you enjoy the game?"

"It was all right."

"Did you play well?"

Brian looked up and blurted out, "We lost, okay? We lost, and it was my fault."

"What do you mean, it was your fault?"

"I let a goal in, didn't I?"

"It was a penalty," Linh-Mai added quickly.

"I dived the wrong way."

"How come? You've played against John Hawler plenty of times. You always know where he's going to shoot."

"Hawler didn't take the kick. It was Casey Dougan."

"Well, him, too."

"I got muddled up with who was taking it. I wasn't concentrating."

Mr. Price stopped stirring. He leaned back against the stove and folded his arms. "Could you see who was taking it?"

"Of course I could see who was taking it."

"Just asking."

"Why?"

"I thought there might be something wrong."

"Like what?"

"Like with your eyes. I've noticed …"

"You said that last summer when we were playing baseball in the garden."

"Yeah, because you kept missing the ball. And now I'm saying it again."

"I told you then — there's nothing wrong with my eyes."

Mr. Price said, "If you say so."

He casually picked an apple from a bowl of fruit on the counter and lobbed it gently toward Brian, saying, "Catch!"

Brian groped for the apple. It brushed against his fingers as it landed on the table in front of him.

Mr. Price said quietly, "I'll make an appointment with the eye doctor."

Brian rose so violently that his chair crashed backwards. He flew out the back door.

Mr. Price started after him, calling, "Brian, wait!"

At the same time Linh-Mai's mother came to the door of her office, the telephone in her hand. "It's Mrs. Anderson, about the job tomorrow. She says she has to talk to you."

"Tell her I'm busy and I'll call back."

Mrs. Nguyen covered the mouthpiece with her hand. "I've told her that already, but she's really insistent."

Mr. Price hesitated at the door.

Linh-Mai offered, "I'll go after him."

"Okay, thanks," said Mr. Price. "Don't let him do anything stupid."

As she left the house, Linh-Mai glimpsed Brian turning from Riverside Drive onto Brunswick Street, the main drag through town, but by the time she reached the junction he'd disappeared. She started toward the town centre, looking on both sides of the street and into the alleyways between the stores. Through one of them she spotted him on the trail beside the river that flowed parallel with Brunswick at the bottom of a steep, grassy slope behind the stores. He was walking slowly now, his hands in his pockets. She saw him stop at a clump of willows and peer up into the branches, his head cocked to one side. Further along he paused to gaze at a group of ducks on the far river bank. She kept parallel with Brian on the road as he continued along the trail, catching glimpses of him between the buildings. When a group of kids appeared in the distance, calling his name, he scrambled up the bank away from them. Linh-Mai knew that would take him to the rear of the Valley Mall car park. She hurried through the big glass doors at the entrance to the mall and jogged past the brightly lit stores, glimpsing Jenna in one of the chairs at Dar's Cuts 'n' Styles. She peered through the rear doors. The evening dusk was made gloomier by gathering clouds, and even with her glasses she found it hard to see if anyone was there. At last spotting movement, she went outside and made out Brian. He was walking toward her through the parked cars.

She called, "Brian."

He looked in her direction, but not at her, his eyes roving. She thought of spotlights sweeping a stage before they locked on to a lone performer. But Brian's eyes didn't seem to lock on to her. He turned and ran. She called again. He stumbled and fell among the cars. She ran to him. He was scrambling up, preparing to take off again.

She begged, "Brian, wait! It's just me." He wiped his face with his sleeve and she asked, "Are you all right?"

After a moment, he said, "The wind's making my eyes water," and started to walk away.

Linh-Mai blurted out, "Do you … do you want to get a pop at the café?"

He said over his shoulder, "Nah, thanks."

"Please. I want to ask you about … about … soccer. I feel

so awful about causing the penalty."

Brian stopped, his back to her. "It wasn't your fault. I keep saying …"

"I know, but … but … suppose it happens again. Suppose the ball comes flying right at my face again?"

Brian turned. "You could try ducking."

Linh-Mai giggled. "I didn't think of that." She started to walk slowly toward the mall, still talking, hoping he'd accompany her. "We have to play St. Croix again and … I'm scared of Hawler." She didn't know what she'd do if he walked away, except feel like a total dork walking across the car park talking to herself.

After a moment's hesitation, Brian followed, saying, "You can't afford to be afraid in defence."

Linh-Mai said, "Yes, but …"

Drifting into step beside her, he went on, "All you have to do is decide you won't be intimidated."

"How do I do that?"

"You balance your strengths against Hawler's."

They reached the mall entrance and Brian held the door open for her. She felt like royalty.

Brian continued, "His strengths are his size and his fierce shot."

Linh-Mai rolled her eyes. "Tell me about it."

They walked slowly past Dollarama and Frenchy's, Brian explaining, "But you have strengths, too. You're quicker than him, and your sense of position is better. That's why you were in the way when he shot this afternoon."

They passed Dar's Cuts 'n' Styles, Linh-Mai sneaking a quick glance at Jenna, who was looking at herself in a hand mirror as one of the hairdressers fussed over her. At the Valley Diner, Linh-Mai bought a bottle of water and Brian got a pop. They made their way past the counter, and the padded stools bolted to the floor alongside it, to the rear of the long, narrow café, where there were a few booths with chrome-edged tables. They sat at a table in the corner, beneath a red neon sign winking the name of the diner. Linh-Mai realized that whenever she'd visited the café in the past, she'd always been with a crowd of her friends. Now here she was alone with Brian, as if they were on a … a … date. She gave a tiny shake of her head, and in order to chase away such foolish thoughts, she said, "Do you think we can beat St. Croix when we play them again?"

Brian said gloomily, "We're going to have to if we want to qualify for the Summer Games."

"I hope they don't get another penalty."

"I can handle it if they do." He looked directly at her as he spoke.

Linh-Mai felt it was a challenge, but she ventured, "I … I … I could tell you who's taking the kick … I mean … if you weren't sure. We could work out a way for me to let you know." He looked away, and she added, "I mean … if that'd help."

He fidgeted in his seat, sipped at his pop and rolled the can between his hands.

She stumbled on, nervous but determined, "I mean … I mean … if you … if it was difficult to see who was taking it." She added, her voice trailing away, "Sorry to mention it."

They sat in silence, sipping their drinks.

Then Brian said quietly, "I can see all right — most of the time."

Linh-Mai nodded encouragingly. "I know."

"But sometimes … things aren't so clear. I get this, like, swirl of colours and dots wherever I look, and I can't see through it." His voice rose suddenly and he kicked the table leg. "It's driving me freakin' crazy." Just as suddenly his voice fell as he went on, almost dreamily, "When I was on the riverside trail just now, I couldn't tell what birds were in the willows, or what sort of ducks were on the river."

She said slowly, "Perhaps … perhaps it would help to do what your dad and Miss Little said, and get your eyes checked. Perhaps glasses would help."

"Glasses are for geeks." He looked at her suddenly — at her glasses — as if he hadn't noticed them before, and said, "Sorry. I didn't mean … yours are cool."

"You could find some that would suit you, too."

He shook his head. "It's different for guys."

She leaned back and folded her arms. That bugged her a bit. She felt sorry for him as he struggled to get used to the idea of wearing glasses, but she'd been through it, too. And while he had the extra worry of wondering how they'd affect his goal-keeping, she'd had to deal with teasing, something she knew he wouldn't have to worry about. She'd survived getting glasses — and so could he. So what was the big deal?

She said, "What do you mean, different?"

He shrugged. "Glasses look good on girls."

"But not on boys?"

"Right."

"That's ridiculous!"

He went on blithely, rolling the pop can between his hands, "Like you. You look …" She was staring at him in her annoyance. He glanced up and their eyes locked for an instant. He looked down quickly, mumbling, "You look pretty in your glasses."

Her annoyance faded at his awkward, unexpected compliment, and she found herself blushing.

He went on, "I was going to tell you, but I didn't want to make a big deal of it, because … because it isn't a big deal. Not for girls."

"But it is for boys?! Come on."

He nodded. "Anyway, goalkeepers don't wear glasses."

He said it so glumly that her irritation melted away, and she said encouragingly, "There's contacts. Mom says I can try them — when she's sure I'll take care of them properly and not tear them or wash them down the sink or something."

Brian muttered, "I suppose, but ..."

He was interrupted by a loud, high-pitched squeal of laughter. It was Jenna, joking with the server at the counter, while she sneaked glances in Brian's direction.

Brian screwed up his eyes and looked around, "Is that Jenna?"

"At the counter — in the red jacket," Linh-Mai said. "She was in the hairdresser's. She's had her hair straightened."

Brian grunted.

Jenna called, "What's up, Flyin' Brian?"

Linh-Mai scoffed inwardly. What right did Jenna have to call him Flyin' Brian? Like she knew anything about soccer.

Jenna went on, as if staking a claim on Brian's attention, "You said you'd be at the mall after the game."

Brian looked at Linh-Mai apologetically and muttered, "I did tell her that. It was after school, and before we went to St. Croix, and ... everything." He called to Jenna, "You've had your hair straightened."

Linh-Mai thought he said it with an effort.

Jenna smoothed her hair. "I'm surprised you noticed."

"Did they straighten up what's inside your head, too?"

Jenna grinned, "Very funny. Come over here and say that."

Brian rose and took a step toward Jenna. He turned back to Linh-Mai and said, "Want to come up to the counter?"

Linh-Mai rose, too, and lied, "I've got to go." She'd sooner live on broccoli for a month than join Jenna at the counter.

Brian said, "Don't … er … no need to tell anyone about —
you know — what I said about not seeing properly."

Linh-Mai shook her head.

"I just want to get through these last two games," he said.
"After that …"

Jenna called, "Are you coming over or what?"

As Linh-Mai left the café, she glanced back. Brian was at
the counter with Jenna, but he was watching Linh-Mai.

9

Dr. Arnold's Prognosis

As soon as Mrs. Nguyen arrived for work the next morning, with Linh-Mai in tow, Mr. Price said, "Reschedule everything planned for this morning, please. I'm taking Brian to the eye doctor."

Brian was at the kitchen table, finishing a bowl of cereal. He glanced up just long enough to catch Linh-Mai's eye.

Mrs. Nguyen asked, "How did you get an appointment so fast?"

Mr. Price winked. "It pays to play hockey with Dr. Brown." He went on, talking fast, "It's probably nothing, eh, Bri? It's just some sort of infection messing up your eyes. But even if it turns out you need glasses, well, look at Linh-Mai here. She's got her new glasses, and she's still playing soccer, and she looks cuter than ever. Right, dear?"

Linh-Mai said, "I don't mind the glasses, but I don't look cute."

"They don't look so bad," said Brian, but he didn't look up.

All morning, as she sat in class, she thought of Brian. She pictured him keeping his eyes wide as Dr. Brown peered into them with the instrument like a flashlight. She imagined him reading the letters on the eye chart, and choosing frames for his glasses, trying on different styles. She expected him to arrive at school around mid-morning, but by noon there was still no sign of him. At first she was amused, guessing he'd delay his return as long as possible, but when afternoon classes started with social studies and his desk was still empty, she was irritated. No doubt he'd expect her to help him out by explaining what he'd missed and telling him what to do for homework. Her annoyance grew in the last class of the day. It was mathematics, and Mr. Cunningham was talking about parallelograms. While the class worked at exercises from their math texts, Mr. Cunningham strolled to Linh-Mai's desk and spoke quietly, nodding at Brian's empty seat, "Could you keep our fidgety friend up to date with his mathematics, please? Take him his homework and maybe go over it with him?" He knew she often helped Brian.

She sighed and said, "No problem."

After class, she packed her homework, and Brian's math books, into her backpack and walked to Riverside Drive. She heard Brian before she saw him. He was kicking his soccer ball against a wooden board in the garden behind his house. It was a game he often played. He'd nailed the board between two trees that grew close together, and the game was to kick the ball against the board and collect the rebound, which sometimes came at unexpected angles.

Linh-Mai stomped up the garden and threw down her book bag. "Hey."

Brian glanced at her and muttered, "Hi." He turned and slammed the ball at the board.

"How d'you make out at Dr. Brown's?"

"Okay, I guess." *Slam* — he smashed the ball against the board again.

"What did he say?"

"Not much." *Slam*.

Linh-Mai drew a deep breath, controlling her growing irritation. "So — when are you getting your glasses?"

"I'm not."

"What? Why?"

He trapped the ball as it rebounded and shouted, "I'm not getting glasses, okay?"

She was suddenly scornful, and her own voice rose until she was as near shouting as she ever got. "Don't get mad at me because you don't want to wear glasses. Do you think it was easy for me facing Cory and Kyle and that crowd, knowing they'd make fun of me? What's so special about you? I suppose it's because you're a guy — is that it — and you're afraid glasses will spoil your image?" She added, surprising herself with her spitefulness, "Or are you just afraid Jenna won't like you in them?"

No answer. Just — *slam*.

She stamped her foot and ranted, "You goofed off for the whole day to get glasses which you're not even going to bother with but you'll still expect me to help you with your homework and probably do it for you!"

After a moment Brian said quietly, "I'm not bothering with them …" *slam* "… because I'm going blind …" *slam* "… and they won't help." As the ball rebounded he trapped it under his foot and stood still, his head down.

Linh-Mai rolled her eyes. "Now you're being ridiculous." She put her hands on her hips, like an exasperated teacher, patience stretched to the limit. "Brian, you're not going blind. You're getting a bit shortsighted, like me, like lots of people. It's no big deal, unless you want to make it one."

He was silent.

She said, uncertainly, "Brian …"

He slammed the ball at the board. It ricocheted past him and came to rest against the side of the house. At the same time he took off, running further into the garden, which sloped steeply to a narrow, wooded ridge.

She stared after him. She felt as if she'd been struck; felt dizzy and thought she might faint. She whispered, "Blind…" She didn't know how long she stood there before she found herself following, and standing at the top of the slope. She could hear stifled sobbing. She followed the sound, threading her way through the trees until they thinned and she was looking out across a flat expanse of marshland to the four lanes of the highway in the distance. A few metres from her, Brian was on his knees, sobbing.

She murmured, "Blind…"

Brian sat back on his heels, sniffed, and rubbed his eyes with his fists. Without looking around, he nodded.

She felt she had to say something, but didn't know what. She said, "You can't be going blind. Is Dr. Brown sure?" and instantly regretted it for its wishful insensitivity. As if Dr. Brown would tell Brian he was going blind if he wasn't sure of it.

Brian sniffed again. "It wasn't Dr. Brown that told me. It was Dr. Arnold. He's a specialist in Saint John. Dr. Brown told me I had to see him and arranged for Dad and me to go straight in. Dr. Arnold said I had an eye disease, and it would make me blind."

Linh-Mai thought, so that's why Brian was away all day. She was ashamed for accusing him of goofing off.

Brian, still sniffing, went on, "We only just got back now. Dad had to take off in a hurry to one of the sites. He said he was going to see Dr. Brown on the way back and ask him about what

Dr. Arnold had said and get a second opinion."

She didn't know what to do. She wanted to make some gesture of comfort but didn't know how. She moved closer to Brian, and reached a hand toward him, behind his back, but withdrew it as he sniffed and caught a sob in his throat. "But ... What did Dr. Arnold mean, blind?" Yet another stupid question, but she stumbled on, "Did he mean blind ... like, you won't be able to see anything at all?" She closed her eyes, imagining blindness as complete, everlasting blackness.

Brian drew a shuddering breath, like a baby exhausted by long crying. "Legally blind is what Dr. Arnold called it. He said I'll be able to see ... a bit, but not much." He added bitterly, "Not enough to play in goal. I asked him."

Linh-Mai moved closer to Brian so that she looked at him in profile. He was staring across the marsh, where the late afternoon sun glinted on the still water. On the far side, two deer grazed beside the highway and they looked up as a logging truck roared past. She wondered, but didn't dare ask, how much of the scene before him he could see. She wondered what being able to see "a bit" meant; how much he'd be able to see as the disease got worse. She tried almost closing her eyes, so that everything was watery and wavy, as if she was looking through a thick net curtain. She looked at Brian, her eyes still almost closed. He was a sort of pink blur. If she didn't know it was Brian, she wouldn't have known who was there. Was that how he would see his friends, and his dad, and her?

10

Garbage

In the week that followed, it seemed to Linh-Mai that Brian's visit to Dr. Arnold might never have happened. When Mr. Price had called at Dr. Brown's office to get a second opinion, the receptionist had said he was away at a conference for a few days, and promised to have him contact Mr. Price as soon as he returned. After that, everything carried on as usual, except that a strange peace took over the Price house as Brian fell into a brooding silence. Now when Linh-Mai called in with her mother in the morning, Brian was ready for school, and they walked there together.

Once, she tried asking, "How are your eyes?" but he said, "What do you think?" so bitterly she let the topic drop. She too resigned herself to silence, thinking how strange and sad it was that she'd wished so often for Brian to walk with her to school, and it had taken a calamity to bring about her wish. On top of that, instead of the happy gossip she'd imagined them exchanging as they walked — about friends and school and teachers and soccer — they seemed doomed to silence.

On Thursday, Mr. Price picked up Linh-Mai and Brian from

soccer practice after school. One of his construction sites was nearby and he stopped on the way home. Knowing he was waiting, Linh-Mai hurried from the changing room and across the playground to the school parking lot.

Mr. Price jumped from his truck, seized her book bag, with her cleats dangling from it, and opened the door. He strode around to the driver's side and climbed in. "How was soccer practice?"

"It was good."

"Did our boy manage okay?"

"Yes. We were mostly practising short passing, so … so he …"

Mr. Price finished for her. "So he didn't have to see much, which is lucky because he can't see much anyway, eh?"

The radio was playing a sad country and western song. Mr. Price tapped his hands on the wheel with the beat. She could tell he was upset, because his drumming was fierce, as if he was angry, or even scared.

When the song ended and the news came on, Mr. Price turned off the radio but kept tapping. Linh-Mai thought of Brian, drumming in the air in math class.

Mr. Price's drumming grew fiercer and he said bitterly, "No, sir. I guess he can't see much."

Wanting to calm him, Linh-Mai said quickly, "He likes playing in goal, doesn't he?"

Mr. Price grinned. "Always did. I tried playing hockey with him when he was a toddler — and all he wanted to do was go in the net. I thought he'd be a goalie and play some serious hockey, like I did, but as soon as he got in school he took to soccer. I was disappointed at first. Wanted him to play hockey, like me, I suppose. But when I saw how much he liked soccer, and how good he was in goal, I didn't mind. It's been good for him.

He can channel all his crazy energy into it. When he gets in goal, all that foolishness disappears and it's like keeping the ball out of the net is the only thing in the world for him."

Before Linh-Mai could say she'd noticed exactly the same thing, Brian emerged from the school, walking slowly and gazing around.

"Suppose he can see us?" Mr. Price murmured. He jumped from the truck and jogged to meet him.

As Brian climbed in, with a small smile at Linh-Mai, she asked, with a glance at his backpack, "Do you have your cleats?"

Brian sighed and shook his head. He set off across the playground.

Mr. Price was climbing in the driver's side. "Where's he off to now?" he asked.

Linh-Mai said, "He forgot his cleats."

Mr. Price drummed on the steering wheel again. He climbed out and checked something in the truck bed, which was loaded with tools and lengths of wood. He climbed back in, but a moment later climbed out and cleaned the windshield. He climbed back in and said, "How can it take so long just to pick up a pair of cleats?"

Linh-Mai said apologetically, "It's a long way to the changing rooms."

Mr. Price sat in silence for a moment, then spoke almost dreamily. "He's got all these posters in his room, posters of famous goalkeepers. His favourite's a picture of Gordon Banks — used to play in goal for England, years ago. Brian says he was the best goalkeeper ever. He's in mid-air, stretched out horizontal, making a save. And every morning, when Brian wakes up — when I go in to wake him, that is — he's looking right at it."

Mr. Price was gazing across the playground. Linh-Mai

wasn't sure whether he was talking to himself or to her as he went on quietly, "It doesn't matter how he falls asleep — what way he's facing — he always wakes so that poster's the first thing he sees. He told me last summer he thought it was fading. That was just before we had the talk when we were playing baseball about him not seeing properly. Since then he's clammed up about it, but I've seen him in the morning, staring at it. First he looks from across his room, then he goes up close, as if he's checking to see if it's fading away." Mr. Price sat in silence for a few seconds before adding, "Let's hope it's just some sort of infection messing up how he sees, because it'll break his heart if it's his eyes that are fading."

He sighed, then jumped from the truck and set off to greet Brian, who had emerged from the school again.

***

In math class the next day, Mr. Cunningham strolled between the rows of desks, pausing when he came to Brian. Linh-Mai glanced across the aisle. Brian had his mathematics book and his scribbler open, and his pencil was poised over the page, but he wasn't moving. He was staring toward the front of the room, but Linh-Mai couldn't tell whether it was at something, or just into a distance that wasn't there. She could see he'd hardly started the assignment.

Mr. Cunningham peered at Brian and said, "I thought you might be asleep."

Brian continued to stare.

"Do you need help?" Mr. Cunningham asked.

Brian shook his head.

The teacher started forward, then stopped. "Are you all right?"

Brian nodded.

"Sure?"

Brian glanced up. "Why?"

"You're so quiet." The teacher smiled. "I never thought I'd say it, but I miss your clowning around."

Brian shrugged and made a show of returning to his work.

As Mr. Cunningham moved on, Jenna turned and whispered, "He means you're boring."

Linh-Mai thought, I miss his clowning around, too. His energy and excitement seemed to have disappeared, as well as the sparkle of merriment in his eyes, which had turned dull and lifeless. She sneaked another look at Brian, and realized he was staring at the banner at the front of the room that promised, *If you can dream it — then you can do it!* She wondered how much he could see of it.

When class ended, and he still didn't move, she tried to stir him from his lethargy, and said, "Hey. What are you thinking?"

She expected a brusque rebuff, but he said quietly, "That poster …"

He fell silent. But she wanted to keep him talking, so she said, "Can you read it … with … you know … your eyes being how they are?"

"I don't have to. I know what it says." His voice changed suddenly, and he said through clenched teeth, "It's garbage."

She thought she could understand his anger. Being a goalkeeper was all he dreamed of. He'd talked about it after Myrna Spigot's presentation. In the middle of joking about the answers they'd improvised when their guest speaker had asked about their dreams, Julie had said suddenly, "But seriously, what do you want to do, like, in the future, after school?"

Brian had said, "Keep goal."

Julie had argued. "You can't just keep goal. You have to earn a living."

"I'll earn a living keeping goal. Dad said he could have earned his living playing hockey if he hadn't got injured, so why can't I earn a living playing soccer?"

Linh-Mai remembered thinking, Why not? He certainly seemed good enough to be a professional goalkeeper. She could imagine him being famous, playing in the Canadian Soccer League, even for Canada. Now, with his deteriorating vision, it was almost an insult to be told that all he had to do in order to achieve his dream was … to dream it.

She tried to defuse his anger. "It's not worth getting upset about."

He muttered darkly, "Isn't it?"

By now all the other students had left the room, and she asked, "Are you coming outside for recess?"

He shook his head.

"Shall … shall I stay in with you?"

"Nah." He looked at her briefly. "Thanks, anyway."

When she returned after recess, the first thing she saw was Myrna Spigot's banner. It had been ripped from the wall and lay in torn, crumpled pieces on the floor. The students already in the classroom were sitting in silence, while Mr. Cunningham stood at the front of the room, his arms folded. Brian was at his desk, his eyes fixed on something, or nothing.

When the second bell announced the start of class, the teacher pointed to what remained of the banner and said, "I would like someone to admit to this act of vandalism because it will save me the unpleasantness of having to interview each of you in turn."

Linh-Mai looked at her desk. She hated it when teachers spoke like this. She felt guilty, and wanted to confess, even if she knew she had done nothing wrong.

A movement at the desk beside her caught her eye.

Brian raised his hand and said, "It was me."

Mr. Cunningham sighed. "Do you mind telling me why?"

"Because what it says is garbage." Brian spat the words again.

Mr. Cunningham said quietly, "The message may be simplistic, but it's well meant, and Ms. Spigot, who was kind enough to share her experiences with you, doesn't deserve this disrespect. Besides, you don't have the right to decide what other people read."

Brian repeated, "It's garbage. It's …"

Mr. Cunningham interrupted, "You and I will talk about it at next recess. Now all of you, take out your social studies books."

Brian took out his text and slammed it on the desk. Mr. Cunningham looked up quickly, but said nothing. Linh-Mai thought, at least Brian seems to be coming back to life.

11

Insulting Behaviour

A week later, as Linh-Mai and her teammates took the field to warm up for the next game in the playoffs — the home encounter with Westfield Ridge — she stayed close to Brian.

The day before, while she was waiting for her mother to finish work, Mr. Price had whispered, "Look out for our Brian in tomorrow's game, will you? Help him get through it. But don't let on I asked you. He doesn't want anyone to know, and I don't want to tell Miss Little, not just yet, in case … well, in case his eyes get better, and then there's no need."

Now she wanted to offer Brian her arm, to be his sighted guide. Over the week, Linh-Mai had been reading on the Internet about the visually impaired, picking up any tips she could find on how to help Brian. But she knew he would reject the help, probably angrily, and she also knew he didn't need it.

Not yet.

She did, however, ask him quietly, "Shall I stay close to goal and tell you which way the ball's coming?"

Brian shrugged. "I'll be okay."

She was relieved that he wasn't mad.

He stood on the goal line and shouted, "Someone try a shot!"

Julie called, slowly and loudly, "It's me, Julie, and I'm shooting … now!"

She kicked the ball gently toward the goal. Brian punted it out to Toby, who lobbed it back, calling, "High one, on your left."

Brian caught the shot easily, looking curiously from Toby to Julie. Linh-Mai looked, too, wondering why they were suddenly treating Brian as if he was a kindergarten kid, or as if he'd never played in goal before, or as if he … couldn't see properly.

Brian rolled the ball to Shay and challenged, "Try your best shot!"

Shay took a fast run up but slowed the swing of his foot as he kicked the ball, so that it dribbled toward the goal. Brian let it go past him and stalked from the net. He set off across the field. Linh-Mai ran after him with Toby, while Shay and Julie hurried across to face him, so that he was surrounded.

He said, "You know I can't see properly! Who told you?"

He looked at Linh-Mai. She shook her head.

"Your dad called," Toby muttered. "He said you were having a problem with your eyes that made it difficult to see clearly, and could I look out for you. He said I wasn't to say anything to you or anyone about it."

Brian looked at Shay and Julie.

"He asked me the same," said Shay.

"And me," Julie admitted.

"Me, too," said Linh-Mai. She shrugged off a pang of jealousy that she wasn't the only one Mr. Price had asked to help Brian.

"I'm leaving," he said. "I'm here to play soccer, not to have a bunch of nursemaids running around after me."

From the side of the field, Miss Little called, "Gather round, everyone."

Shay said, "Sorry, Bri."

Linh-Mai added, "We were just trying to help."

"I don't want help," Brian snarled.

Julie put her arm round his shoulders and Toby coaxed, "Come on, Bri."

They steered him to where the teams were collecting at the side of the field. A crowd of students and parents from both schools was already gathering behind the team benches.

Miss Little started, "I don't have an inspirational message like Ms. Spigot …"

She looked at Brian and smiled. Linh-Mai was relieved to see him smile back. He'd escaped serious punishment for tearing down Myrna Spigot's banner. Mr. Cunningham had kept him in for a couple of recesses during which, Brian said, he'd lectured him on self-control. The incident seemed to have jarred him from his despair in time for the game with Westfield Ridge.

Miss Little went on, "but I want to remind you to play your best."

"We need a win," Steve interrupted. "If we don't win today we may as well give up because we won't get to the Summer Games."

"There's still a chance if we tie — or even if we lose," Jillian protested.

"We'd just have to win the return game against St. Croix," Jessica explained.

"That's what I mean," said Steve grimly.

"Suppose we end level on points," Toby suggested.

"Then the team with the most goals will go through," said Miss Little.

"So Steve's right," said Shay. "We need a win — and we need goals."

"And we have to stop them from scoring," Steve added. He looked hard at Brian.

The Westfield Ridge team jogged onto the field.

"Let's go," said Shay, preparing to lead Brunswick Valley out.

Brian hung back. "I want you to substitute me, please, Miss Little."

"But we don't have any substitutes."

"Then I'll play another position, and someone else can go in goal."

The Brunswick Valley players looked at one another, their faces clouded with worry. Linh-Mai was worried, too. Brian never gave up, never backed down. It wasn't like him. And without Brian in goal, Brunswick Valley seemed somehow wrong — and horribly vulnerable.

"What's up, Bri?" asked Jessica.

Brian didn't answer.

Shay, with a glance at Brian, said, "He can't see properly."

Miss Little nodded, as if she had been expecting to hear that, and put her hands on Brian's shoulders. "Is that what you want?"

Brian nodded.

"I could take Brian's place," Toby volunteered. "Then he could play fullback."

Linh-Mai felt a thrill of excitement at the thought of Brian playing alongside her. It would be far easier to help him then; to be his guardian and his guide.

As they took the field, a high-pitched voice rose above the hubbub of the spectators, calling, "Bri-an."

"Is that Jenna?" Brian asked, surveying the growing crowd with narrowed eyes.

"In the pink jeans and powder blue jacket, to the right of our bench, at the front," said Linh-Mai. "She's waving you over."

"She can wave all she likes," Brian scoffed, turning his back.

Linh-Mai sneaked a glance in Jenna's direction. When it was clear Brian was ignoring her, she turned and pushed her way back through the crowd.

Steve groaned, "Oh no."

"What's up?" Shay asked.

"My uncle's here." Steve pointed to a man in a green track suit pacing on the sideline as if he was coach of one of the teams. "He's staying with us for a few weeks because he quit his job and he needs time to find himself, Mom says. He thinks he knows everything there is to know about soccer — and he's a jerk."

"Ignore him," Shay advised. "Let's concentrate on winning."

From the beginning of the game, Linh-Mai felt herself under triple threat. For starters, she was still trying to get used to playing in her new glasses. In addition, she didn't have Brian behind her in goal, taking charge of the defence, telling her which balls to go for and which to leave for him, when to tackle and when just to screen, when to go forward and when to hang back. And, finally, she was used to having Toby beside her at fullback, slow, but dependable — and fully sighted. Now she had Brian as her partner in defence, and she quickly realized that not only was he unfamiliar with playing at fullback, but his vision had deteriorated even more than she thought.

She'd taken her usual position on the right side of the goal, and Brian had assumed Toby's position on the left. The first time Westfield Ridge attacked down the right side, Linh-Mai moved out to cover the approaching forwards — and found Brian close beside her. She told him to stay on the left in case the attack switched to that side. The same thing happened again not long after, and again she told him to stay on his own side. The third time it happened, halfway through the first half, the Westfield Ridge forwards, realizing Brian was out of position, suddenly swept the ball across the field. Linh-Mai raced across to cover for Brian, and found him racing with her, so that now the right side was open. She wheeled around to regain her usual side as the advancing forwards passed back, but again found Brian with her. She felt as if they were in an old silent movie, racing comically and frantically backwards and forwards. With a desperate sliding tackle, she managed to block a shot by one of the Westfield forwards, and the ball trickled to Toby, who scooped it up gratefully.

The Westfield Ridge supporters had been laughing at the spectacle of the fullbacks scrambling to and fro. Linh-Mai could ignore them — but blushed as she thought of the Brunswick Valley students and parents watching. She was glad her mother and Mr. Price hadn't arrived yet. Mrs. Nguyen had promised to bug Brian's father to finish work early so that he could come for the second half, and bring her, too.

A harsh shout came from the side of the field. "Sort your-selves out in defence, Brunswick Valley!" It was Steve's uncle, who stood with his hands on his hips, shaking his head, as he scolded, "You're playing like a bunch of primary kids."

A high, speculative ball from a Westfield midfielder sailed toward Brian. He went to clear it but the ball glanced off his foot to Toby, who flung himself on it. Then, trying to intercept a low shot by the visiting centre forward, Brian missed the ball completely, and Toby only just managed to stick his leg out and poke it clear of the goal.

Steve's uncle jeered, "Do you need glasses, fullback?"

Linh-Mai stole a glance at Brian. His eyes were fixed on the ground.

A few minutes later, a Westfield Ridge corner kick bounced through the cluster of players in the penalty area and rolled to Brian. He looked around, his eyes roving among the players waiting near the halfway line, and kicked the ball upfield. It landed at the feet of an opposing midfielder.

"Good pass, fullback!" Steve's uncle shouted sarcastically. "Would you like me to bring you a plate? Then you can put the ball on it when you give it away to the other side."

At halftime, Linh-Mai whispered to Brian, "Don't get mad, but ... how much can you see?"

"Enough."

"Can you see the ball?"

He said sharply, "Are you responsible for how I play?"

She held up her hands. "I'm just asking."

She started to walk away. But he spoke from behind her, his tone softer, and she stopped.

"I can see the ball when it's not too distant, but it's hard to judge how fast it's coming. It's like one second it's far away, and then suddenly it's right there, travelling faster than I thought."

Remembering Brian's wayward pass, Linh-Mai asked, "Can you see people?"

"'Course I can see people."

"I mean, can you make out who they are?"

Brian shook his head.

"Can you see colours?"

"A bit, unless they're close together, then they get muddled up."

"What about shapes?"

"Sort of."

The next time Brian prepared to pass the ball, soon after the start of the second half, Linh-Mai called, "Left — tall, thin, blue!"

Brian kicked the ball successfully to Julie, who passed to Shay. He kept the ball close to his feet, twisting and turning to avoid the tackles of the Westfield midfielders. In the centre, Steve was surrounded by three defenders. Shay slipped past another tackle and set off across the field in a diagonal run, leaving the Westfield midfielders behind and drawing Steve's defenders with him. Suddenly, he spun around and, catching Steve's eye, passed into the space left by the defenders. Steve collected the ball and fired it past the goalkeeper.

The Brunswick Valley supporters clapped and cheered.

Steve proclaimed, "We're on our way to the finals!"

"Maybe. *If* we keep the lead for the last fifteen minutes," Shay cautioned.

Linh-Mai and Julie hugged, while the twins danced in triumph.

Brian, staring up the field, asked, "Did we score?"

Buoyed by the goal, Brunswick Valley kept attacking, and Linh-Mai told Brian, "Move up. Stay parallel with me."

Steve sent in a hard shot, which the goalkeeper pushed around the post for a corner. Shay took the kick, arcing the ball high toward Steve, who chested it down neatly and slammed it at the corner of the goal. It hit the post and rebounded to Jillian, who fired it back. This time the goalkeeper caught the ball and quickly kicked it out, over the heads of the Brunswick Valley forwards and past the midfielders who had moved up to support the attack. Already the Westfield forwards, who had retreated to help protect their goal, were racing into Brunswick Valley's end of the field.

Linh-Mai called, "High ball coming toward you, Bri."

He stood motionless, as if unaware of what was happening in the game. Linh-Mai was about to call again when she realized he was concentrating fiercely, his eyes roving, his face tense with the effort of estimating the speed and height of the ball.

"I see it," he said.

Linh-Mai moved behind Brian in case he missed the ball. He went to head it, but it glanced off his shoulder and landed where she had been standing. One of the advancing Westfield forwards passed it to the centre forward. Toby was left unprotected. He took a few uncertain steps from the goal line. The centre forward chipped the ball over his head and into the net, leaving him on his back where he had fallen after he jumped despairingly for it.

Julie put her head in her hands. Steve kicked viciously at the ground, cursing. Linh-Mai looked at Brian. His shoulders slumped, his head hung, and his whole body seemed to sag.

She ran to him and said, "I should have stayed in position."

Brian said, without looking up, "I thought I had it covered."

Julie hurried across. "You nearly got it."

"We were caught out," said Shay." We should have been back faster to help you."

Toby lumbered up. "I should have stayed in the net."

Steve joined the group. Linh-Mai wondered what she could say to protect Brian from Steve's scorn, but the Brunswick Valley centre forward just said, after a moment's hesitation, "Tough break."

From the sideline Steve's uncle shouted, "Wake up, fullback. You're playing like you don't care."

Steve rolled his eyes.

"What's wrong with you, fullback?" Steve's uncle ranted on. "Are you blind?"

Linh-Mai turned and shouted, "Shut up, snot face!"

She caught a glimpse of Mr. Price in the crowd. He had been moving toward Steve's uncle. He stopped, grinning.

Referee Cline ran across and held up a yellow card. "You can't talk to spectators like that, young lady, no matter what the provocation. You get a caution for insulting behaviour and for using rude language."

Linh-Mai said, "But ..." Her teeth were clamped tight, her fists were clenched, and her arms were rigid by her sides. Julie put an arm around her shoulders and turned her away from the referee, while Shay protested, "That's not fair."

As they lined up for the kickoff, Brian caught Linh-Mai's eye and whispered, "I can't believe you said that."

Linh-Mai smiled and looked away. When she glanced back a few seconds later, she found he was still looking at her.

Ten minutes after Linh-Mai's outburst, the game ended with the score still 1-1.

Brian trudged from the field. Linh-Mai was about to follow when Referee Cline called her over. "I'm sorry I had to caution you for telling that spectator to ... er ... to be quiet."

Linh-Mai started, "So why ..."

Referee Cline held up his hand. "I insist on mannerly play at all times, so I simply can't allow players to be rude to spectators." He grinned and added, "Even when they deserve it." He watched Brian, walking ahead of them, for a moment, and said quietly, "I'm not sure what's going on with your gifted goalkeeper friend, although Miss Little has given me a hint or two, but it's good to know he has a staunch and brave friend like you to help him." He patted her arm and walked away.

Linh-Mai followed Brian to where Mrs. Nguyen and Mr. Price were waiting beside the field. Mrs. Nguyen clapped as they approached, and Mr. Price said, "Well played, you two."

Brian mumbled, "I screwed up."

Mr. Price put his arm around Brian's shoulders. "You played your best. That's what counts." He winked at Linh-Mai.

"Remind me not to get on your wrong side."

Linh-Mai looked at him, puzzled. "What do you mean?"

"I'd be afraid of what you might call me."

Linh-Mai blushed. "I wouldn't be rude to *you*."

Mr. Price said gently, "I know that, dear. I'm teasing. I just want you to know I'm proud of you for sticking up for our Brian like you did. I'm glad he's got a brave friend like you."

Linh-Mai thought, that's two people calling me brave in two minutes. She protested, "I wasn't being brave. I just couldn't stand listening to that man's stupid comments anymore."

Mr. Price insisted, "You acted on behalf of a friend, without considering the consequences. That's bravery."

Linh-Mai's mother nodded and smiled. She asked, "Do you two want a ride home? We can wait while you change."

Brian looked at Linh-Mai and raised his eyebrows.

She said, "We'll walk, thanks."

12

Second Opinion

Linh-Mai and Brian strolled slowly homeward, still in their blue soccer uniforms, their cleats slung over their shoulders. They lingered on Brunswick Street, looking in the store windows, then cut between the buildings and scrambled down the grassy slope to the riverside trail.

Brian mumbled, "What Dad said about you …"

Linh-Mai interrupted, "All I did was tell someone to shut up."

"That's what I mean. Thanks for … sticking up for me … for being, you know, a friend."

Linh-Mai said, "Brian, I've always been your friend." Then, to break the awkward silence that followed, she pointed to a small flock of ducks on the river and said, "What sort are they?"

"Describe them."

"They're white, and they've got a black patch on their heads and on their sides."

"They're eiders."

"There are some dowdy brown ones, too."

"They're the females. The males are always more glamorous than the females."

Linh-Mai said, "Liar."

"It's true." He smirked, "Same as humans."

She punched him lightly on the arm.

He pointed across the river and said, "Is that another eider, on the riverbank?"

Linh-Mai laughed. "It's an old piece of newspaper." She stopped abruptly and said, "Sorry." She glanced quickly at him, afraid that she'd offended him by laughing at his mistake. She found he was looking critically at her. With sudden insight she thought, the way Brian sees me now will be the way he'll always see me. For him, it'll be like I'm always nearly thirteen. Even when we're really old — like, thirty or more — he'll still see me as I am now.

She said, "What?"

"I really like your glasses."

She offered tentatively, "Do you want to try them, just to find if glasses might help you see better?"

"They wouldn't."

"You just don't want to wear glasses."

He shook his head. "Dr. Arnold said glasses wouldn't help, neither would contact lenses, not with what's wrong with my eyes."

"But you have to do something. You can't just say, okay, I'm going blind."

"Why not?"

"Because you have to fight it. Because it's not fair. Because you should hang on to being able to see for as long as you can." As they climbed the slope and emerged on Riverside Drive, she concluded wistfully, "I thought with glasses perhaps at least you could keep goal until the end of the season."

Brian said, "Nah," adding, "Anyway, Dad still thinks it's just an infection, and my eyes will get better when it clears up."

Linh-Mai couldn't decide whether she heard hope or desperation in his voice.

Once they got back to Brian's house they sat in the kitchen where Mr. Price set a snack of chocolate chip cookies and milk in front of them. Almost immediately there was a quiet knock at the door.

Dr. Brown entered saying, "My receptionist told me you wanted to see me as soon as I got back."

Mrs. Nguyen put her head around her office door and told Linh-Mai, "Come in here."

Mr. Price said, "No need. You and Linh-Mai, you're like family." He turned to Dr. Brown, talking quickly. "Brian's eye problems are going to clear up by themselves, right? That Dr. Arnold doesn't know what he's talking about. Just because he's a big-shot city doctor, and we're from Brunswick Valley, he thinks he knows everything and we don't know our eyes from our elbows. Brian's just got a bit of an infection, eh? I used to get itchy eyes when I was a kid, and I couldn't see properly for a few days, but it always cleared up by itself. I told Dr. Arnold I'd get a second opinion. I don't think he understands …"

Dr. Brown interrupted gently, "I'm afraid it's not an infection, and it won't clear up by itself. Brian has to learn to live with a serious eye problem."

Linh-Mai glanced at Brian. His face betrayed no emotion. His eyes seemed fixed on something in the distance, like they had at school, although there was no distance in the crowded, cluttered kitchen.

Dr. Brown went on quietly, "Dr. Arnold will want to do some more tests, but he's fairly certain that Brian has something called Leber's — Leber's Hereditary Optic Neuropathy, if you want the full name."

"He's got what?" Mr. Price spluttered, dropping heavily

into a seat at the table beside Brian. "Leber's Hereditary … what …?"

Dr. Brown sat at the table, too, saying, "It's a disease. It won't go away — Brian has to accept that, you too — and Dr. Arnold is the best person to treat it." He turned to Brian. "I'm sorry to bring bad news. Do you want to ask me anything about Leber's?"

Brian asked in a small voice, "What will happen to me?"

"The disease will seriously affect your eyesight."

"How?"

"Like it has already, but I'm afraid it will get worse."

"How … worse?"

"You'll be able to see less and less, until eventually you will be, as Dr. Arnold said, what we call legally blind."

Brian still gazed into the distance that wasn't there.

His father burst out, "Why … where … how did he get it? Did he catch it from someone?"

Dr. Brown shook his head. "It's hereditary, as the name suggests."

"But I don't have it — do I?"

"No. It's passed on by the mother."

Mr. Price muttered, "I might have known."

Dr. Brown said, "I can offer some hope." He reached across the table and squeezed Brian's arm. "Legally blind doesn't mean totally blind. You'll be able to make out shapes, and you'll mostly be able to get around by yourself. You might even be able to ride your bike — carefully, with your friends, like Linh-Mai here, around to guide you. And remember that people with vision problems still take part in sports."

"There you go, Bri," Mr. Price put in. "We've seen them on TV, eh?"

Dr. Brown went on, "You can also keep in mind that a few

— a very few — people with the type of Leber's that Dr. Arnold thinks you have do get somewhat better, although they are still significantly … er, handicapped."

Brian repeated quietly, "Handicapped."

An image surged involuntarily into Linh-Mai's mind, of the kids at school who had teachers' assistants hovering over them all the time. Was that how Brian would be? She knew he'd hate that.

Dr. Brown fluttered his hands at his sides. "I'm sorry to have to tell you this. You know I'll help all I can." He looked at Mr. Price. "Meanwhile, do keep the appointments with Dr. Arnold. He'll want to do some more tests, and he can suggest the best course of treatment."

"But it's not going to help much, right?" Brian demanded.

After a pause, Dr. Brown admitted, "It will help. But, no, not much."

"And glasses or contacts won't fix things?"

"No. Sorry." He squeezed Brian's arm again. Then he rose and looked at Mr. Price. "Call me if you need to talk again."

Mr. Price said, "But he'll still be able to play in goal, won't he?" He nodded hopefully — yes — in response to his own question, until he saw Dr. Brown's sad shake of his head.

When Dr. Brown had gone, Brian continued to gaze at nothing. Linh-Mai's mother looked from Brian to Mr. Price, slowly wringing her hands. Mr. Price stared at the table. Several times Linh-Mai saw him raise his eyes toward Brian and then lower them. He leaned forward, his fists on the table, and opened his mouth as if he was about to speak, but said nothing.

Linh-Mai watched Brian from the corner of her eyes.

When Brian had told her he was going blind, the shock of it had been so severe, so sudden and so horrific, that she had thrust it aside like an awful memory she wanted to erase, in the same way that Brian and Mr. Price seemed to in the week following their visit to Dr. Arnold. She marvelled at how she — not to mention Brian and his father — had been able to carry on living "normally" with the knowledge of Brian's encroaching blindness always *there*. She remembered the time in grade three when an older boy had made her life miserable by lying in wait for her as she walked home. He always demanded the remains of her lunch money, threatening to cut her hair off if she told anyone. Through all that time — it was weeks before she told her mother — she carried on as if everything was all right, managing to be happy at home and in class and on the playground, but always knowing *something was wrong*; that her happiness was an illusion. Now she realized that her efforts to help Brian — by guiding him through the soccer match, and by talking lightly about wearing glasses — had been a way of creating a kind of illusion of normality, a way of setting aside the seriousness of his condition. Suddenly, with Dr. Brown's quiet, gentle statement of the fact that Brian would be handicapped — a handicapped, legally blind person — she felt the illusion disappear, and when she looked at Brian, it was as if she was looking at him in a new world, a world in which Dr. Arnold's prognosis had turned him into a different being.

If he was no longer Flyin' Brian, Brunswick Valley School's fantastic goalkeeper, then who was he? Would he still be disorganized and restless and exuberant? Would he still drive the teachers crazy, with his shuffling feet and drumming hands and clowning around? Lately there had been no trace of the foolishness and the high spirits. If these were disappearing along with Brian's vision, then who would be left?

So strong was her sense of the impending loss of her friend, Flyin' Brian, that she clasped her hands together under the table, holding on to them in case she gave way — embarrassingly —

to her yearning to put her hand on his arm, to hold on to him, to stop his transformation into someone she wouldn't know.

Just when Linh-Mai began to wonder whether they would sit forever in silence, her mother suggested, "I'll make us some tea, shall I?"

Mr. Price sighed, "Yeah." At last he looked at Brian and said, "We'll cope. You'll get by. You're a fighter, like me, right? And we can get help to teach you how to ... manage ..." His voice trailed off.

Linh-Mai had never before heard the tick of the clock on the kitchen wall.

Brian murmured, "What will you think of me?"

Mr. Price said, "What do you mean?"

"What will you think of me when I can't play in goal?"

"I'll think just the same as I do now."

"But you always said my goalkeeping was what made you proud of me."

"It is ... was.... But there are lots of other things to be proud of."

Brian looked bleakly at his father. "Like what?"

Mr. Price said, "Well ... er ..."

Linh-Mai's mother turned from making the tea and rested her hands on Brian's shoulders. "There's your bright and cheerful personality for a start," she said, bending down and kissing him on top of his head.

Mr. Price added, "Yeah — and your smiley face, and the way you make us laugh, at the same time as you drive us crazy."

Brian looked at Linh-Mai. She thought for a moment and suggested, "Your mathematics?"

Brian managed a ghost of a smile.

13

Winning Is Not Important

As Linh-Mai walked to school with Brian the next morning, she imagined she was Brian's sighted guide, although she was careful not to betray her desire to help. When they arrived, they checked the soccer bulletin board and found a notice from Miss Little announcing: *Team meeting after school today — in my classroom.*

"It'll be about how we're going to play against St. Croix tomorrow," said Linh-Mai.

"And about who's going to play in goal," Brian added. "Dad called Miss Little last night. I said to tell her I couldn't do it anymore because of the Leber's. I said he could tell her about it — but no one else."

"Everybody knows something's wrong with your eyes," said Linh-Mai. "They just don't know what."

"I'll explain when I tell them I have to give up soccer."

"You don't have to give up soccer. And I still think you should play in goal."

Brian shook his head firmly.

"Just one last time?" she pleaded.

This was a repeat of the conversation they'd had the night before. After Dr. Brown's visit, Linh-Mai had stayed to help Brian with his mathematics, showing him what he'd missed because he'd been unable to see the chalkboard. Mr. Price had papers strewn across the kitchen table, so they'd worked in Brian's room. When they finished, Brian had looked around at his posters of famous goalkeepers and said, "I may as well take these down now."

"Why?"

"I'm giving up soccer. I can't be a blind goalkeeper."

"You could still play, and you could still dream about being a famous goalie."

"You mean dream about it, like Myrna Spigot said — dream it and it'll happen, like magic?" Brian said sarcastically.

"No. Of course not. I meant, like, imagine it, daydream it, for fun, like you might dream about being rich and famous."

"Why? There's no point when it's impossible."

She'd pleaded with him to play in goal against St. Croix.

He'd refused, and now he said again, "No!"

***

At the end of the last class, as Linh-Mai and her friends headed off for the meeting, Jenna called to Brian, "I'm going to hang out at the mall. Are you coming?"

Brian said, "I've got a soccer meeting."

Jenna pulled a face. "Bo-ring."

Brian walked on, and Jenna called after him, "I'll be there for a while."

"Okay."

"So … are you coming down after your stupid meeting?"

"Don't know. Probably not."

Linh-Mai caught Brian's eye and he muttered, "Like, *definitely* not."

Jenna tossed her head. "Suit yourself."

They set off for the primary classrooms, trooping through the hallways of the old school, looking at the student writing and artwork on the walls as they went. Despite the displays, the bright yellow walls, and the laminated banners with messages like, "Be the Best That You Can Be," the hallways were still dismal and gloomy, and it was a relief to arrive at Miss Little's kindergarten, with its big windows where the sun poured through on bright afternoons.

Miss Little waved them in and said, "Sit where you like."

Linh-Mai paused at the door, taking in the alphabet train across the top of the chalkboard, the playhouse at the back of the room, the paint-smeared easels in the art centre, the carpeted reading corner with Miss Little's big chair, the cubbies stuffed with building blocks and puzzles and scraps of material. She followed her friends in, feeling awkward and huge among the little tables and chairs, and beside the low hooks, hung with a few shiny book bags, forgotten at the end of the day. The smell — paint, crayons, wet clothes and pee — carried her back to when she was in kindergarten, and she remembered how she'd loved it.

Steve and Brian lowered themselves carefully into the kindergarten chairs, while Toby, Shay and Julie sprawled on the rug in the reading corner. Linh-Mai joined them.

Miss Little started the meeting with, "We're level on points with Westfield Ridge, and three points behind St. Croix. Therefore, if we win tomorrow, we'll finish above Westfield and level with St. Croix."

"What happens then?" asked Steve.

"Then the team with the most goals will go on to represent the province in the Games next summer."

Toby said, "So, even if we beat St. Croix, they'll still be the ones, because they've scored more goals than us."

"Yes — unless we can not only beat them, but beat them by three goals," said Miss Little. "I don't mean we simply have to score three goals. We have to be *in the lead* by three goals."

Steve whistled. "We've never beaten St. Croix by more than one goal."

"And they usually beat us," Julie added gloomily.

"It's a tall order," Miss Little agreed. "But," she looked around the room, "I think we can do it, don't you?"

Miss Little was famous at Brunswick Valley School for her optimism. Linh-Mai remembered it from when she was in kindergarten. Even when the class had behaved badly all day, before they went home Miss Little would say, "Tomorrow you'll be the best-behaved class in the world, won't you?" And as they all chanted, "Yes, Miss Little," Linh-Mai was quite sure they would be.

So now she was almost convinced by Miss Little's optimism — until she remembered they'd be without Brian in goal, and then she wasn't so sure. Her teammates, however, were infected by Miss Little's determination. Toby muttered, "Yeah!" while Steve punched the air and the twins high-fived one another.

Miss Little's voice stilled the hum of excitement. "As well as being important, tomorrow's game will also be a kind of celebration." She paused before adding, "It will be a celebration of Brian's last game with us."

There was a moment of surprised silence, broken by Jillian. "Are you moving away, Bri?"

Slumped in the little chair with his legs stretched in front of him, Brian shook his head.

Miss Little went on, "I mean it will not only be Brian's last game with us, but his last game of soccer. His father called me last night, with Brian's permission, and asked me to explain why — unless you want to explain for yourself, Brian."

"I've got something called Leber's Disease," Brian started, sitting up, his hands on his knees. "It affects your eyes, and … and … you gradually lose your sight, most of it, anyway. I can't see much already. You probably noticed."

"Your dad said you were having a bit of trouble with your eyes," said Toby. "He didn't say you were...." He stopped.

"Going blind," Brian supplied.

The team was silent.

At length Julie said, "Why didn't you tell us before?"

Brian shrugged. "I thought the eye trouble would go away." They fell silent again, until Brian went on, "I don't want to leave you with only ten players on the team against St. Croix, so I'll play somewhere — somewhere I won't do too much harm. But I've decided that'll be my last game."

"But you can still see enough to get around, and to follow the play, can't you?" said Shay.

"Sort of. But I can't tell one person from another. That's why I let the penalty in against St. Croix. And I can't judge how fast the ball's coming at me, and that makes me slow."

"We wouldn't mind you being slow," said Julie.

"I'm slow and nobody minds," said Toby. He looked around. "Do you, guys?" No one spoke, and he muttered, "Well thanks, guys."

Shay asked, "When did you decide to stop playing, Bri?"

"It was in the last game, when I missed that high ball. Someone in the crowd shouted out that I was playing as if I didn't care."

Steve scoffed, "That was just my stupid uncle. Don't take any notice of him."

"But it made me think," said Brian. "Not being able to see properly had the same effect on me as not caring. I felt I was letting you all down, not being able to do my part for the team. I don't want to play if you have to look after me — like you were in the last game."

"But no one minds looking after you," said Miss Little.

"*I* mind," said Brian.

After a few beats of silence, Steve said quietly, "It won't seem right without you in the net."

"I think you should be goalkeeper one last time," Julie suggested.

"That's what I tell him," said Linh-Mai.

Brian shot her a warning glance and shook his head firmly. "I'll play to make up the team, but I won't play in goal. I'd lose the game for you."

"Very well," said Miss Little. "We'll have to change positions, like we did for the last game. Now, let's talk about how we're going to play against St. Croix. We have to go all out for goals, so we'll play with five forwards, and I want the midfielders to …"

Linh-Mai shuffled across the rug so that she could whisper to Brian, "I still think you should play in goal."

Brian looked down at her and shook his head.

Linh-Mai kneeled beside him and insisted, "Yes!"

He whispered back, fiercely, "No!"

"But you're our goalkeeper. You're Flyin' Brian."

"Not anymore."

"Who cares if we lose the game?"

"Everyone cares."

"It's more important for you to play in goal for your last game!"

Linh-Mai looked around. Her voice had risen in her effort

to sway Brian, and everyone was staring in her direction.

She stammered, "Sorry, Miss Little."

"Linh-Mai's right," said Shay. "If it's Brian's last game — then he should play in goal, like he always has."

"I'm telling you: if I play in goal, I'll lose the game for you, and Brunswick Valley's chance of representing the province next summer," Brian protested.

"Winning the game's not the most important thing," said Shay. "Not this game, anyway."

14

Swan Song

Linh-Mai paused at the top of the bank above the back field, looking down at the teams warming up amid cries of encouragement from the spectators who were already clustered on the sidelines and streaming in from cars lining the Back Road at the far side of the field.

She felt surrounded by gloom, behind her the dirty brick of the old school, in front the sombre green of the spruce woods that pressed in at both ends of the back field and covered the low hills that lay between Brunswick Valley and the sea. Grey clouds scudded across the sky, driven by a chill wind blowing in from the ocean, stirring the trees and whipping the corner flags against their posts. In the lowering evening light of late fall, the players, in their blue and purple uniforms, looked like exotic birds let loose to strut and preen.

She was last on the field because Miss Little had called her back as she was leaving the dressing room to tell her, "We need you to play more as a midfielder than a fullback today. Get upfield to support the forwards in every attack, while Toby will stay back as sweeper. But we can't afford to concede a goal, so you're also going to have to get back to help him — and Brian, of course, because you know best the condition of his eyes, and how much he can see." She'd smiled, warning, "You'll be run ragged."

Linh-Mai was pleased that Miss Little saw her as Brian's special helper.

She caught the scent of the ocean as she pulled wind-strewn strands of hair from her eyes and hurried down to the field, where she joined Toby and Shay, who were firing weak shots at Brian in goal.

The news that this would be Flyin' Brian's last game, and rumours about why, had spread through both Brunswick Valley and St. Croix. Brunswick Valley's supporters lined the school side of the field — Linh-Mai glimpsed her mother and Mr. Price among them — while the visiting supporters had gathered on the far side.

Behind the Brunswick Valley goal, Miss Little's kindergarten class was lined up in the care of parents. Brian had been the children's guest speaker earlier in the year during Active Living Week, when his manic energy, as he jumped and dived across the classroom demonstrating how he kept goal, had delighted the young students. Miss Little told him later they thought he was just a big kindergarten kid. Now they waved with wriggling, chubby fingers whenever he looked in their direction, and every time he leaped in goal, they cheered.

Miss Little and the St. Croix coach, Mr. Pellerin, shook hands, took their places behind the team benches, and called the players together.

As Miss Little reviewed the strategies they'd discussed earlier, Linh-Mai overheard Mr. Pellerin tell his team, "We don't need to do anything spectacular. We don't even need to win. As long as we don't lose by more than two goals, we're through to the Summer Games. So the pressure is on Brunswick Valley.

They'll be attacking frantically, so I'll expect our forwards to help out the defence." He looked at Hawler and Dougan before going on, "We may even grab a goal, because the Brunswick Valley backs will be up supporting the forwards, making their defence vulnerable to a quick breakaway. And don't forget," he looked around sheepishly, "their goalkeeper has ... problems. Take advantage of them if you can." He looked at Hawler and Dougan again.

They nodded, and Hawler grinned.

The teams lined up to take the field. St. Croix led the way, Mr. Pellerin booming the players' names and positions through a megaphone as they trotted forward. At the name of John Hawler, the St. Croix supporters clapped and shouted, "Hawler the Mauler!" and "Smash 'em, Hawler!"

With Miss Little at the megaphone introducing her players, Shay led the Brunswick Valley team out, to the cheers of the home supporters and some boos and jeers from the St. Croix crowd. When it was Linh-Mai's turn and Miss Little called, "At fullback — Linh-Mai Nguyen," half of her wanted to become invisible, while the other half exulted, proud to be a part of the spectacle and the glory of the event.

Brian was last, and as Miss Little announced his name the shouting stopped and all the spectators, from home and away, applauded. Some had brought blankets and had made themselves comfortable on the ground, and many students were sprawled on the damp grass, but all scrambled up and stood, clapping, as Brian headed toward his goal.

Linh-Mai had lingered after taking the field so that she could walk to the Brunswick Valley end with Brian.

As they passed Hawler, the big St. Croix striker threatened, "This is the day I get one past you, Flyin' Brian." He turned his voice into a sneer as he said "Flyin'."

Brian stopped and faced him. "It'd be the first in two years."

Hawler predicted confidently, "But today's the day."

Linh-Mai muttered, "Come on, Bri."

The Mauler looked hard at him, staring right into his eyes, before Brian turned away. Linh-Mai fell into step on one side of him, and Toby on the other, as if they were his bodyguards. They took their positions in defence. In front of them, Shay and Julie, who had been standing close together, moved apart to cover the midfield. Julie turned and flashed a brilliant grin at Linh-Mai, holding two thumbs up. Steve waited for the referee's signal to take the kickoff, the ball at his feet, and the twins close on each side.

The Brunswick Valley crowd chanted, "Raise your voices. Make a din. Brunswick Valley — win, win, win!"

From across the field the St. Croix supporters started a rival chorus: "St. Croix get the goals — and Brunswick Valley rolls!"

The referee whistled for the game to begin.

For the first fifteen minutes, Linh-Mai felt as if she were playing with training weights attached to her ankles and wrists. She felt weighed down by the importance of the game, the importance of winning it for Brunswick Valley School, for the parents and students supporting them, and, above all, for Brian, so that his last game with them would be a memorable one. She thought her teammates felt the same way, because, like her, they were moving and passing and tackling in a kind of deliberate, dreamlike state. St. Croix seemed to be infected by the same mood of caution and restraint, and Linh-Mai thought the teams were like two dogs, sniffing cautiously at one another, unsure how to behave. Even the spectators seemed influenced by the mood, their cries of support, so enthusiastic before the game, now fewer and quieter.

Then everything changed.

Linh-Mai intercepted a tentative shot by one of the St. Croix midfielders and passed carefully out to Shay, who was near the halfway line. He rolled the ball under his foot, surveying the field as Hawler and Dougan steamed toward him. He sashayed calmly past Dougan, avoided Hawler equally easily, and slid the ball on to Jessica. She passed across the St. Croix penalty area to Jillian, whose shot hit the crossbar. As the ball bounced back toward Steve, he turned around and, falling backwards, scissor kicked it past the astonished goalkeeper into the net.

The home supporters erupted in a frenzy of cheering. The kindergarten kids behind Brian's goal danced and shouted, "Bri-an! Bri-an!" although so far in the game he'd had only one save to make, an easy catch from a corner kick. Miss Little beamed, Linh-Mai's mother flung her arms in the air, and Mr. Price shouted, "Let's have another!"

The goal seemed to release the Brunswick Valley players from their self-imposed caution, and suddenly they were playing with a fluidity and confidence that had been missing from their game all season. Linh-Mai wondered: Was it because up till now they had been ruled by caution, their play inhibited by their fear that Brian's goalkeeping was, strangely, no longer as secure as it always had been? Was it because they'd truly taken to heart her argument that winning was not important in this game, so that they were simply *playing*, with a carefree delight that inspired them? Or was it, simply, for Brian? Whatever the reason, she thought, if they'd played like this all season, they would not have been in this desperate fight now, where they had not only to win against their old rivals, but win by the seemingly impossible margin of three goals.

St. Croix, meanwhile, fought back strongly, goaded into their usual aggressive style of play, and with their supporters now roaring their team on.

But it was Brunswick Valley that struck again. After half an hour, Shay once more kept the ball while he waited for his forwards to find an open space. He caught Steve's eye and gestured at three St. Croix defenders who were advancing on him. Steve nodded and moved behind them. Shay waited while the defenders converged on him, then slipped the ball between them. As they turned on Steve, Shay ran ahead, collected Steve's quick return pass, and tapped the ball past the goalkeeper.

As Brunswick Valley kept up the attack through the first half and into the second, Linh-Mai's thoughts moved beyond delight in how well they were playing to speculation that perhaps, after all, with just one more goal to score, they might make it to the Summer Games.

She dealt easily with a speculative pass into the penalty area by a St. Croix midfielder and, with Hawler advancing on her, slipped the ball to Toby. He passed it out to Shay. Remembering Miss Little's instructions to support her forwards, Linh-Mai moved upfield. Shay passed back to her and pointed to the wing. She raced up the side of the field with the ball but found her way barred by Dougan.

Trapped near the corner flag, she thought first to lob the ball over him, but he was too close and too tall. Julie and Shay were close by, jockeying for position among the St. Croix defenders, trying to create space for her to pass into. Linh-Mai went to run around Dougan but he stepped in front of her. She bounced off him, winded, but kept her feet, and lunged for the ball. Dougan went for it at the same time. He slipped as he swung his foot at it and his boot smashed into her shin. She tottered forward with the ball, struggling to catch her breath, only to find Hawler about to challenge her. She sidestepped, but he moved with her.

As her weight landed on her injured ankle, it gave way and

she careened further sideways. He hustled after her. She fell to her knees and the burly St. Croix striker, unable to stop, fell over her. She picked herself up and stumbled on. She heard Shay call, "Here!" and glimpsed him standing unmarked in front of the goal. She shaped to pass, but Hawler, with a roar, shoulder-charged her from behind.

She sliced the ball, and the force of his tackle, coupled with her momentum, sent it rocketing not toward Shay, but toward the net. The St. Croix goalie dived but couldn't hold the ball, which rebounded in Linh-Mai's direction. Unable to draw breath, and with her ankle buckling under her, she fell headlong. As her face and her glasses ground into the mud, she felt the ball bounce against the top of her head. She lay sprawled on the ground for a moment, gasping for breath and overwhelmed by pain.

When she pulled herself to all fours, she found her glasses dangling around her neck, bent and twisted. One lens lay in the dirt. She raised her head and looked for Shay. She needed to apologize for slicing the pass so disastrously wide of him.

She found him beside her, and started, "Sorry …"

Then she heard the cheers of the Brunswick Valley supporters. At the other end of the field, Toby and Brian were performing a crazy dance, while on the sideline Mr. Price was shouting, "Go, girl!" and her mother was jumping up and down and waving her arms.

She stood uncertainly. Julie bounded over to her and hugged her.

Linh-Mai asked, "What happened?"

"You scored. You headed a brilliant goal."

"I did?" She saw the goalkeeper still spread-eagled on the ground, and the ball in the back of the net, and said, "Mom's going to be mad about my glasses."

The St. Croix coach called a time out.

Linh-Mai limped to the bench, where Miss Little felt her ankle and said, "You'd better miss the rest of the game."

She protested, "I'll be all right."

Her mother pushed her way through the crowd.

Before she could speak, Linh-Mai said, "Sorry about my glasses."

Mrs. Nguyen waved the apology aside. "I'm not worried about your glasses. I'm worried about *you*."

"I'm all right, really." She wobbled to her feet, keeping the weight off her injured ankle. "See?"

Her mother took her glasses and said, "How will you manage without these?"

Mr. Price arrived at the bench and said, "Let's take a look." He bent the frame roughly back into shape. Julie produced the missing lens, which he snapped into place. He held the glasses up and the lens fell out. He snapped it into place again and produced a roll of electrical tape, which he wound around each side of it.

As he worked, she asked, "How come you have a roll of tape in your pocket?"

"You never know when you're going to need it."

"Like for what?"

"Like for mending glasses that get broken in soccer games," he said, handing them back. "That should get you through the rest of the game."

She tried them on. They sat crookedly on her nose, and felt loose, and one side pinched her ear. She said, "Thank you. They're perfect."

While Miss Little beamed at her team, saying, "You have the three goal lead that will take you to the Summer Games! Now you have to hang on to it." The Brunswick Valley crowd chanted and cheered, but still Linh-Mai heard the St. Croix coach's raised voice: "What's wrong with you? ... Pathetic display ... Attack! ... Still need only one goal ... Brunswick Valley defence is weak ... Wisp of a girl and an overweight slowpoke ... Goalkeeper with serious — I mean *serious* — problems ... Take advantage ..."

When the game resumed, St. Croix attacked furiously. With Brunswick Valley dominating, Linh-Mai had been able to venture well past the halfway line, with only Toby and Brian behind her, ready either to intercept a St. Croix counterattack, or to receive a pass back. But now she found herself pinned near her own goal, defending desperately.

Each attack left Toby, beside her, exhausted and gasping for air, his hands on his knees. Jessica, who had dropped back to help the defence, was carried off the field after tackling Hawler, leaving Brunswick Valley with only ten players. Then Julie collided with Dougan and was left limping so badly that she could hardly play.

Brian had been called into action only a few times while Brunswick Valley stayed on the attack, but now he was suddenly under pressure. As Hawler let fly a hard, long shot, Linh-Mai saw Brian's eyes roving wildly. She called, "High in the left corner," and he leaped to save. A few minutes later Dougan fired the ball in and Toby warned, "Low to your right." Brian fumbled the save but managed to steer the ball wide of the goal.

St. Croix surged forward again and Hawler broke through the defence to shoot from point-blank range, but Brian, rushing from his goal line, somehow managed to block the shot with his feet. The ball fell to Dougan, who, with Brian still on the ground, fired it straight back. Linh-Mai, watching helplessly, shouted, "Right, low," and Brian threw himself across the goal to parry the shot.

It was, Linh-Mai decided, his swan song, a legendary performance as thrilling as a swan's beautiful, final song was said to be. She thought, Brian is having his best game ever, but we'll never see him play in goal again. How unfair it seemed for Brian to have so much goalkeeping talent, only to have it become useless.

Then, forcing her mind back to the game, she thought: We're weathering the storm. We've almost made it!

But even as the thought entered her head, St. Croix attacked yet again and Toby, backpedalling before Hawler, slipped and stumbled. The St. Croix striker watched him fall before carefully tapping the ball toward him. Toby tried to get out of the way but the ball bumped against his arm.

Hawler turned to the referee and demanded, "Penalty, ref!"

Shay, rushing up, protested, "He didn't mean to handle it."

Hawler said, "Tough."

Referee Cline pointed firmly to the penalty spot.

Linh-Mai watched as Dougan and Hawler hovered over the ball. She could see Brian's eyes roving from one to the other. She tried to edge forward so that she was closer to him and could tell him who was going to shoot, but the referee motioned her out of the penalty area.

At the last moment, Dougan stepped back and Hawler, with three quick steps, blasted the ball with his right foot high toward the left corner of the goal. Brian, who had been dancing on the goal line, soared across the goal and caught the ball.

At the next break in play, Linh-Mai whispered, "How did you know which way to dive?"

"Easy," said Brian. "I knew Hawler would take the penalty, he's so desperate to score past me."

The sounds from the crowd mirrored the action of the game, the home supporters falling silent with each St. Croix attack, and breathing a relieved "Aaaah" as Brunswick Valley cleared the ball, while the visiting supporters roared into a crescendo of excitement as St. Croix went forward, and groaned at each repulse.

Linh-Mai and Toby had given up telling Brian where the ball was coming from because he seemed to divine it somehow, as if his skill at reading the game made up for his loss of vision. Often they didn't have time to warn him, anyway, so great was the speed and ferocity of St. Croix's offence.

When, at last, Miss Little held up five fingers to signal that they had to hold on for only another five minutes, Linh-Mai had grown so accustomed to the rhythm of attack and repulse that she assumed it would continue until the referee whistled for the end of the game — and they were through to the Summer Games. So it was almost a shock when Steve suddenly burst through the St. Croix midfield and headed for the visitors' goal. The St. Croix defenders, who had been supporting their forwards, raced back to bar his way, and finding himself without support, Steve paused, keeping possession of the ball.

On the sideline, Miss Little waved her arms, urging the Brunswick Valley defenders to move up. Linh-Mai recalled her telling them in training sessions, "The best way to defend is to attack. You can never afford just to sit back and let them come at you. If you're on the attack, they won't be."

Suddenly Linh-Mai found her team in the same confident formation that had been so successful in the first half, the midfielders pressing up behind the forwards, while she was poised near the halfway line ready to join the attack, with just Toby and Brian behind her. Hawler was lurking nearby, the only St. Croix forward who hadn't retreated into defence.

Linh-Mai watched him closely, telling herself, if Hawler gets the ball, and turns their defence into attack, I can cut him off easily; and even if he gets past me, there's still Toby and Brian behind me.

But it was Dougan, not Hawler, who put St. Croix on the attack again when he intercepted a pass from Jillian, eluded Steve and barged past the limping Julie. Shay called, "Get back!" as he raced to challenge Dougan. Toby was already moving out to bar Hawler's way, so Linh-Mai ran behind him in order to form a second line of defence. Glancing over her shoulder as she ran, she saw Shay catch up with Dougan and prepare to tackle. At the last moment, Dougan dipped his shoulder, swerved, and charged into Shay. Both crashed to the ground. As he fell, Dougan swung his foot and nudged the ball on to Hawler, who had been waiting for Dougan as if they were in a relay race.

Hawler took over the attack, veering toward the wing and drawing Toby further from Brian's goal. He slowed as Toby confronted him. He feinted to move to Toby's right, but passed his foot over the ball and steered it the other way. Toby spun around, trying to stay with the centre forward, but one foot caught in a rough patch of turf. His leg twisted and he collapsed with a groan. Hawler gathered speed again. Linh-Mai glanced upfield. Shay was still on the ground. Julie was limping slowly back. Steve and Jillian were running to help but had gotten only as far as the halfway line. Meanwhile, Toby had risen but had instantly fallen back to the ground, clutching his knee. Linh-Mai was the only one between Hawler and Brian. She moved quickly toward Hawler, to try and force him wide of the goal. He was watching her, and seeing him hesitate, she gathered speed.

From behind, she heard Brian call, "What's going on?"

She turned and called over her shoulder as she ran, "It's Hawler, going for the right …"

Then she collided with the hulking St. Croix striker. She fell heavily and the back of her head smashed against the ground with the kind of dull force she knew meant that the impact would take a moment to resolve into pain. She closed her eyes as it struck. When she opened them, Hawler had stopped a few metres past her. He was watching Brian. Steve and Jillian were still running desperately, but to Linh-Mai they looked as if they were struggling through soft sand, clawing desperately to pull themselves forward. Shay had at last risen from the ground and was limping painfully behind Julie.

The crowd had fallen silent.

Brian stood in the centre of the goal, holding his arms out in front of him. Linh-Mai thought, with a forlorn pang, like a blind person.

Hawler frowned. He prepared to shoot, but stopped and cocked his head, glancing toward his coach.

Mr. Pellerin in turn looked at Miss Little and in the silence Linh-Mai heard him say, "It's your call."

Linh-Mai thought, We've won! We're through to the Summer Games! Mr. Pellerin knows it wouldn't be fair for Hawler to score like this, with Brian unable to see.

Mr. Price was standing near Miss Little. As she caught his eye, he shrugged and nodded slowly.

Miss Little murmured to the St. Croix coach, "Play on."

Mr. Pellerin gestured to Hawler, pointing at the goal.

And Linh-Mai understood.

It would be unfair to everyone, even Brian, to let his disability prevent the goal. She glanced at Brian, still searching for the ball, and told herself, things are different now. He's getting better at paying attention and his eyesight is getting worse. That's how it is. But he's still Brian — the eye disease is a part of him now. They should have known this — they did know this

— when they asked him to play goal one last time.

The St. Croix centre forward tapped the ball toward the goal. The soft thud of his boot against the ball seemed to echo around the back field. Brian whirled in Hawler's direction as the ball rolled past him and into the net.

Hawler moved closer.

Brian said, "It's you. You scored. You finally got one past me."

Hawler took Brian's hand, shook it, and held it. He said quietly, "I guess only because you couldn't see, old buddy." He led Brian to where Linh-Mai still lay, her head thudding, and said, "Let's help your friend up." Bending down to Linh-Mai he added, "Sorry, little girl. I tried to avoid you but you just kept coming at me."

15

Because We're Friends

Linh-Mai and Julie didn't bother to change. They gathered their belongings, stuffed them into their backpacks, and paused by the mirror to inspect themselves as they hurried from the girls' changing room.

Julie said, "D'you suppose we should clean ourselves up, just a bit?"

"We haven't time," Linh-Mai reminded her. "Miss Little said to hurry, and the others are waiting for us."

Julie laughed. "You look as if you've been in a fight."

"So do you," Linh-Mai said.

Their soccer socks hung around their ankles, showing their knees, which were raw and scratched and embedded with dirt. Julie's forehead was smeared with mud from one fall, and her left cheek was scuffed and red from another tumble. Linh-Mai's glasses, held together with Mr. Price's tape, sat askew her nose, one lens white with scratches. Her face was still pale from the jolt to her head and her hair was caked with mud on one side.

Referee Cline had blown his whistle to end the game moments after Hawler's goal. Linh-Mai, with Brian and Toby supporting her, had been last off the pitch, behind Shay and Julie, who, both limping, had helped each other from the field, arms around one another's shoulders.

Miss Little, leaning forward with her hands clasped in front of her and her eyes shining, had said, "I'm so proud of you." They'd had to wait by the field while first their coach, then their parents, made sure their injuries weren't serious. It had taken Linh-Mai several exclamations of, "I'm all *right*, Mom!" before Mrs. Nguyen had believed her. Then Miss Little had hugged them one by one and reminded them, "We're going to Pizza Café to celebrate the end of the season. I'm going straight down now to make sure they're ready for us. Follow as soon as you can."

Shay and Toby were waiting at the school gate.

"Where's Brian?" Linh-Mai asked.

"I saw him heading down to the back field a while ago," Toby volunteered.

They walked around the school and stood at the top of the bank above the back field in the gathering darkness. Brian was in one of the goals, his gaze lingering on the field before him. In silence, they walked down the bank and stood behind the goal. At the other end of the field, a young deer wandered from the woods.

Toby whispered, "Look at the deer."

Brian murmured, "I can't see it."

Linh-Mai wasn't sure whether he was talking to himself or to them.

Toby bit his lip. "Sorry. Stupid thing to say."

"Can't you see it at all?" Julie asked Brian quietly.

He shrugged. "Now I know it's there I can make out a sort of blur, but that's all."

Toby laughed suddenly. "That's what Hawler said you

were, remember, when you made that save on him last year. He thought he had the goal because you were flat on the ground from making another save, so he just tapped the ball toward the net, but you went flying across and saved it. He stood there shaking his head saying, 'How d'you move so fast? You were just a blur.'"

Julie giggled. "He called you something else that time you saved when he was through the defence and all by himself. There was no one back to help you, so you rushed way out of your penalty area to tackle him, but he got past you, and he thought he'd left you behind, but you chased him into the penalty area and got the ball by diving through his legs. He stood over you with his hands on his hips and said, 'You crazy b...'"

"What about that time you sprained your finger saving against Westfield Ridge last year?" Linh-Mai recalled. "They came straight back at us before you could get treatment, and there was another shot, and you couldn't use your hands because your finger hurt too badly, and the ball was too high to kick out — so you saved with your head."

"Your best save ever was that one against Bethel Station," said Shay. "Remember? The Bethel centre forward shot low and you dived for the ball but it hit a rock and deflected upward so you turned your dive into a cartwheel and saved it with your legs."

Julie laughed, "Everyone applauded you, even the Bethel players."

Toby said softly, "I remember that one. It was, like, the greatest save I've ever seen." Something in Toby's voice — a catch — made Linh-Mai glance at him. His lip was trembling. "I always thought I'd see you in the soccer roundup on TV someday."

Brian said, "Nah. No more goalkeeping."

Shay clapped him gently on the shoulder and said, "Good-bye, 'keeper. Hello, coach!"

This was something Miss Little had proposed.

She'd been waiting by the main door when Linh-Mai and Brian had arrived that morning, and she'd greeted Brian with, "I was watching English Premier League soccer on television last night when I had a great idea! You could be like Chris Coleman, who coaches Fulham. He played for Wales until he was in a bad car accident that ended his playing career. But he didn't just give up soccer. He took up coaching." Miss Little's eyes had shone with excitement as she went on, "You could be my assistant coach. You could even take over from me and be coach of the Brunswick Valley School soccer team! Then, when you're older, you could be coach of one of the big teams in the Canadian League — Toronto All Stars, or North York Astros."

Brian had murmured a doubtful, "Maybe," but Linh-Mai had caught him smiling secretly a few moments later.

From the side of the school, Steve called, "Are you guys coming?"

Brian didn't move.

Linh-Mai said, "Bri?"

"I'll be along in a minute."

They paused at the top of the bank until Brian at last turned slowly and started after them.

They found the rest of the team waiting by the school gate, where Steve had stolen a scrunchy from one of the twins and was holding it over his head while they jumped to retrieve it.

Steve shouted, "Shay! Catch!" and threw the scrunchy toward him.

Jillian called, "Stop him, Julie."

Julie threw her arms around Shay's neck and clung to him.

While they wrestled, Toby picked up the scrunchy and danced with it, holding it tantalizingly aloft. The twins turned on him.

Linh-Mai was about to join in on the girls' side, but hesitated, afraid that Brian would be unable to join the friendly melee, and would feel left out. He was on the other side of the schoolyard, walking slowly with his head down. As she looked back, she noticed Mr. Price close by in the shadows at the foot of the steps by the main door.

He looked from Brian to the roughhousing friends and murmured, "Will he be all right? Does he need me to stay and look out for him?"

Linh-Mai, not knowing how to answer, not even sure whether he was talking to himself or to her, hovered uncertainly.

The twins were attacking Toby, swinging from his neck while he dangled the scrunchy in the air. Shay wrenched free from Julie, and Toby threw the scrunchy to him. As he caught it, Julie threw herself at him again and he passed it to Steve, who took off out of the school gate, waving it over his head. The others chased after him.

Mr. Price seemed suddenly to become aware of Linh-Mai, and muttered, "You'll see he gets to the pizza place, will you? And see he gets home safely?"

She stepped into the shadows beside him and whispered, "Yes," as Brian approached.

"You'll take care of him, eh?"

"Yes." Another whisper.

Mr. Price murmured, "I don't want him to know I'm, like, worrying about him. He doesn't want that." He loped up the steps, eased the door open, and slipped stealthily inside.

Brian peered into the shadows where Linh-Mai waited. "Who's that?"

She moved into the light. "It's me."

"What are you doing?"

"Waiting for you. I thought we could walk to Pizza Café together."

"I don't need looking after."

"I know."

"Why are you waiting then?"

"Because we're friends. Come on. Let's catch up with the others." Linh-Mai jogged forward.

Brian said, "Wait. I … I can't see too much when it's dark like this."

She held her hand toward him.

He hesitated, took it, and they set off together.

Other books you'll enjoy in the Sports Stories series

Soccer

❏ *Miss Little's Losers* by Robert Rayner #64
The Brunswick Valley School soccer team haven't won a game all season long. When their coach resigns, the only person who will coach them is Miss Little … their former kindergarten teacher!

❏ *Corner Kick* by Bill Swan #66
A fierce rivalry erupts between Michael Strike, captain of both the school soccer and chess teams, and Zahir, a talented newcomer from the Middle East.

❏ *Just for Kicks* by Robert Rayner #69
When their parents begin taking their games too seriously, it's up to the soccer-mad gang from Brunswick Valley School to reclaim the spirit of their sport.

❏ *Play On* by Sandra Diersch #73
Alecia's soccer team is preparing for the championship game but their game is suffering as the players get distracted by other interests. Can they renew their commitment to their sport in order to make it to the finals?

❏ *Suspended* by Robert Rayner #75
The Brunswick Valley soccer form their own unofficial team after falling foul to the Principal's Code of Conduct. But will they be allowed to play in the championship game before they get discovered?

❏ *Foul Play* by Beverly Scudamore #79
Remy and Alison play on rival soccer teams. When Remy finds out Alison has a special plan to beat Remy's team in the tournament, she becomes convinced that Alison will sabotage her team's players.

Track and Field

❏ *Fast Finish* by Bill Swan #30
Noah is fast, so fast he can outrun anyone he knows, even the two tough kids who wait for him every day after school.

❏ *Walker's Runners* by Robert Rayner #55
Toby Morton hates gym. In fact, he doesn't run for anything — except
the classroom door. Then Mr. Walker arrives and persuades Toby to join
the running team.

❏ *Mud Run* by Bill Swan #60
No one in the S.T. Lovey Cross-Country Club is running with the pack,
until the new coach demonstrates the value of teamwork.

❏ *Off Track* by Bill Swan #62
Twelve-year-old Tyler is stuck in summer school and banned from watching TV and playing computer games. His only diversion is training for a
triathlon race … except when it comes to the swimming requirement.

❏ *Mud Happens* by Bill Swan #82
Matt wants to change schools so he can be coached by the head of a team
of elite runners. But is there such a thing as too much, too soon?

Hockey

❏ *Interference* by Lorna Schultz Nicholson #68
Josh has finally made it to an elite hockey team, but his undiagnosed type
one diabetes is working against him — and getting more serious by the
day.

❏ *Deflection! by Bill Swan #71*
Jake and his two best friends play road hockey together and are members of
the same league team. But some personal rivalries and interference from
Jake's three all-too-supportive grandfathers start to create tension among
the players.

❏ *Misconduct* by Beverly Scudamore #72
Matthew has always been a popular student and hockey player. But after
an altercation with a tough kid named Dillon at hockey camp, Matt finds
himself number one on the bully's hit list.

Roughing by Lorna Schultz Nicholson #74
Josh is off to an elite hockey camp for the summer, where his roommate,
Peter, is skilled enough to give Kevin, the star junior player, some seri-
ous competition, creating trouble on and off the ice.

❏ *Home Ice* by Beatrice Vandervelde #76
Leigh Aberdeen is determined to win the hockey championship with a new, all girls team, the Chinooks.

❏ *Against the Boards* by Lorna Schultz Nicholson #77
Peter has made it onto an AAA Bantam team and is now playing hockey in Edmonton. But this shy boy from the Northwest Territories is having a hard time adjusting to his new life.

❏ *Delaying the Game* by Lorna Schultz Nicholson #80
When Shane comes along, Kaleigh finds herself unsure whether she can balance hockey, her friendships, and this new dating-life.

❏ *Two on One* by C.A. Forsyth #83
When Jeff's hockey team gets a new coach, his sister Melody starts to get more attention as the team's shining talent.

Basketball

❏ *Out of Bounds* by Gunnery Sylvia #70
Jay must switch schools after a house fire. He must either give up the basketball season or play alongside his rival at his new school.

❏ *Personal Best* by Gunnery Sylvia #81
Jay is struggling with his running skills at basketball camp but luckily for Jay, a new teammate and friend has figured out how to bring out the best in people.

Baseball

❏ *Hit and Run* by Dawn Hunter and Karen Hunter #35
Glen Thomson is a talented pitcher, but as his ego inflates, team morale plummets. Will he learn from being benched for losing his temper?

❏ *Power Hitter* by C. A. Forsyth #41
Connor's summer was looking like a write-off. That is, until he discovered his secret talent.

❏ *Sayonara, Sharks* by Judi Peers #48
In this sequel to *Shark Attack*, Ben and Kate are excited about the school trip to Japan, but Matt's not sure he wants to go.